Table of Conten

Chapter 1

"Your mom and I are moving abroad for a job opportunity…" I walk through the terminal and find my gate. I plop down in a random seat and pull out my sketchbook to pass the time. "I know it's your senior year so going overseas for your last year in high school is not ideal…"

I have an aisle seat on the plane, which is nice for going to the bathroom, but not nice when the people next to you need to go. Luckily the flight isn't too long. "We are giving you the option to come overseas with us, or my friend from Ohio has offered for you to stay with him for your senior year…"

I grab my bag off the conveyor belt after we land; it's not too big since I had the majority of my stuff pre-sent to the house. I wheel my luggage to pick-up and see a tall man in a baseball hat waving to me. He's wearing an Ohio University T-shirt with plain cargo shorts. He gives off a friendly vibe as he runs over and takes my belongings.

"Michelle! It's so great to finally have you!"

"Thank you, Mr. Owens. And thank you for taking me in on such short notice."

"It's no problem! And hey, you can call me Paul!" He walks and talks at a pace I struggle to keep up with. To me, we're sprinting, but to him, it just seems like a casual stroll through the park.

"Thank you, Paul." I try not to sound out of breath as I follow him out of the airport and into the parking lot.

"So, am I correct to assume your father told you about how you would be working around the house? I will pay you, of course…but I just need…"

Paul goes on and on about my household chores. That was the agreement my parents and I had about me staying in the States. If I wanted to stay in America, I would work for their friend, since there was no way in hell I was going to move to a new country for my senior year of high school. Also, any excuse to get away from my parents is a great one.

Paul lost his wife recently and hasn't been able to keep up with the housework, said my father, so he agreed to let me stay with him if I helped take care of the housework. Honestly, I think I'm getting the better end of this bargain, especially with Paul paying me. He seems like a nice straightforward person, so I'll do my best to help.

"So, are you sure you're okay with starting fresh at a new school for your senior year? I thought part of the reason you didn't want to go abroad was because you'd miss your friends."

I chuckle, not only at the question but also at Paul's slight Southern accent. "That's not the reason. Also, I don't have friends." I notice how my comment makes Paul a little uncomfortable—his smile slowly fades and he has this pitying look in his eye. "But, I'm hoping to make friends at this new school!" I try to put on my 'look how positive and gung ho I am!' demeanor. I guess I'm able to convince him since his smile quickly returns.

"I'm sure you will! My boys will help you make friends in no time!"

"Boys?" I ask, genuinely confused.

"Yeah sure, my boys, Sam, Charlie, and Zach. They're triplets, the same grade as you. They're mighty excited to meet you! Your dad mentioned them, right?"

No. Of course, he wouldn't have. "Umm, I guessed I missed that…" I try to lightly laugh it off but honestly, I'm pissed. How could he leave out such an important detail? I'm going to be living in and cleaning up a house of not one person, but *three* sons? I knew this deal was too good to be true. He totally didn't tell me on purpose.

"Oh, you'll love them, great boys, very friendly and popular!" Paul is so chipper after every word. I just sit there and nod. "But don't think about dating any of them, they're known to be heartbreakers." He lets out a loud laugh that startles me. I awkwardly laugh along. "I'm just kidding, he Hehe."

"Haha…yeah, you don't have to worry about that…" I don't think he hears me say that last part; he's still laughing over his joke. I just sit and gently laugh with him.

He spends most of the hour-long car ride telling me about his three pride-and-joys. Sam is the oldest of the triplets, Charlie is the middle, and Zach is the rebellious youngest. I honestly zone out during most of the conversation—I'm enamored with the scenery we're driving past. Living in Philly all my life, I'm used to tall buildings, smog, and homeless people outside my window; but here, there's nothing but fields of greens and yellows. Small flowers bloom near the road and far in the distance, small houses can be seen peeking out during the drive. I want to paint the scenery as soon as possible.

"And here we are…" Paul makes a turn onto a long driveway. It's so long I can't even see the house, just a bunch of trees. There are also not a lot of other houses nearby; I think I remember seeing about five of them in the last fifteen minutes.

Finally, I see the house. It's your stereotypical American two-story house with an extra little window at the top for the attic. It's a plain white color with matching white windows. The only thing that has color is the deep red door. It's very different from the broken-down apartment building we lived in.

Paul leads me up the porch while telling me all about the new renovations they had done on the house. "You see this porch is a newer one we put in, more stable." He stomps his foot down on the gray boards to show it won't break. "And those chairs are actually handmade by Sam." Paul motions to the black rocking chairs that are nestled on each corner of the porch.

"He made them himself?"

"Oh yeah, Sam's real creative, it seems like yesterday he was making birdhouses…and now he's making furniture and even a guitar for Charlie."

"Wow, he seems really talented." It's reassuring to know I won't be the only artist in the house.

"Now then, let's get you settled in." Paul opens the door to reveal the chaos inside.

It's quite the contrast to the pristine outside appearance. As soon as you open the door you are stepping on old newspapers and disregarded mail. The front door leads immediately to the staircase, which is littered with dirty clothes, plates, and food wrappers.

"Sorry for the mess…" Paul can barely hide his embarrassment. "Here, I'll show you around…"

To the right is the living room. I immediately notice the dust on the coffee table and game consoles. As we walk around the dirt-covered couch, I notice a few stains on the rug. "Do you have any pets?"

"Ah, no. We used to have a dog, but when she died we were so heartbroken we couldn't get another one."

I sigh a breath of relief that those stains are not from a dog. Then again, they could be that old. We reach the dining room next. You can't even see the table anymore underneath all of the dirty dishes and papers. I notice Paul looking away in embarrassment. If his wife died a year ago, is that the last time this place was cleaned? The kitchen isn't any better. The tabletops are stained with all sorts of dried-up food. The dishwasher is coated in a thin layer of dust, meaning no one has touched that thing in a while. The sink is filled with rotting food and dishes—I have to cover my mouth because of the smell. There is a window looking out to the backyard over the sink. It's a vast field with trees in the distance. Only a single trampoline and fire pit are taking up the space. In Philly, I didn't have a yard or anything, so I feel a bit of jealousy and frustration looking out at their yard.

"This door right here leads to the basement." Paul's voice leads my attention from the backyard to an adjacent door. "We don't use it much other than for storage, but you'll find the laundry machines and cleaning supplies in there." Paul's face reddens. "I'm sorry for the mess; your dad said you'd do it for free, but my guilty conscience couldn't let you do this without some pay."

I smile at him and say, "No big deal!" but inside I'm rolling my eyes at my father's words. Of course he would say I'd do it for free.

The last room is an office space. Just a computer and hundreds, maybe even thousands, of papers all around. "I hope you have your own laptop—this here is our only computer and it has maybe fifty viruses on it." Paul laughs like it's a joke, but something inside me tells me it isn't.

We make our way back to the front door. "Anyway, you should have a good three hours before my boys come home, they're at a party to celebrate the new school year. Oh, and I left your school schedule up on your bed. You'll be in the attic." My first thought is, *great, I'm going to be Cinderella here*, but as he leads me up the messy stairs and we walk by the toxic-looking bathroom, he talks about how much work he and his boys put into making the attic homely. Another flight of stairs leads me to a door with my name on it. Literally. They made a wooden sign with my name neatly carved on it. "Sam made it for you…he made most of the furniture in your room." Hearing that makes me feel a little more relieved.

I open the door and immediately feel the soft carpet under my shoes. I examine the purple floor and see no stains whatsoever. I look around and am astonished at how clean the space is. They kept the wooden walls the same but added a ceiling fan with hanging lights attached to it. Directly under the fan is a queen-sized bed with dark purple bed sheets and matching pillows. On either side of the bed are deep brown nightstands. I take note of how smooth the corners are and how glossy the finish is. Sam has a lot of talent. The last thing in the room is a large dresser stationed next to the window. The dresser looks to be about six feet tall and is adorned with six shelves. And that's it. The rest of the room is empty. My face lights up and my heart starts racing.

"Your mom recommended we leave space for your art projects; she said you were a painter and liked having your weasels and papers set up."

I smile as I walk around the open space. "It's actually called an easel and I use canvas to paint… But thank you, this is amazing!"

Paul smiles. "Your mom also said your favorite color is purple. Your dad said blue but I went with her choice."

I smile back at him. "I'm glad you listened to my mother." Paul nods and winks at me, and I start to feel reassured about staying here.

"Now then, I'll start moving your stuff up here. I've been keeping your shipped stuff in my room so the boys didn't go poking around. Why don't you start cleaning before those rascals come and distract you?"

I nod towards him. As much as I would like to rest for a bit, and he probably knows this, if he's asking me to start cleaning now that's a warning. If I don't have the house clean by the time his sons come home, I might never get it clean.

I thank Paul and go into overdrive. In the basement, I find everything I need. Mop, broom, bleach, brush, gloves, trash bags, and all the chemicals in the world. I roll my eyes. "Honestly, if they had all this then why is the house such a mess?" I don't give myself time to think that over and get started.

One by one empty wrappers, broken dishes, and unidentified materials go into trash bag and clothes go into the washer. I dump an entire bottle of bleach on the ground just to get the gunk off. I mop, scrub the carpet until all stains are nonexistent, and wipe every surface at least ten times. After almost four hours, the inside of the house starts to look more homely, but still needs a lot of work. I begin wiping down smaller things before taking on the dishes, and that includes photos. In the dining room, three professional photos of three young boys hang on the wall. I get a good look at my roommates for the next year.

In the photo, they all look to be about sixteen or seventeen so they must have been taken in the last year or so. The first photo includes a boy with deep blue eyes and short dirty blond hair. His hair looks neatly combed and his smile is brightly cheerful like Paul's. I can tell he got his looks from his father. The next picture shows a boy with dark brown eyes and curly black hair. His skin is paler than the other boys and he's wearing a black hoodie and black beanie to match. He chose not to smile in his picture. The last picture has a more muscular boy. His skin is the tannest of the three and he has the same hair and eye color as the first boy. But unlike the first boy, his hair is longer and wavey. He reminds me of those hot lifeguards you see in old

Baywatch movies, running shirtless on the beach with tiny red shorts. I feel like I have a sense of who they are from the photos, but I don't want to make any assumptions until I meet them.

There is one more framed photo in the dining room. It's a smaller photo resting on a windowsill, a wedding photo. The woman standing with Paul is beautiful with big curly brown hair and dark brown eyes. I'm so mesmerized by the happy couple in the photo, that I don't hear Paul sneak up behind me.

"That was the best day of my life." I swing around to face him.

"Oh, I…"

"The house looks wonderful! I almost forgot we had floors!" Paul laughs as he admires the room. I want to say something about his wife, but I just can't find the words. "I moved all of your boxes to your room, plus your luggage from the car. Since it looks like you finished most of the house, why don't you go upstairs and start to unpack?"

"Thank you, Paul! But I still haven't started on all the food and dishes piled in your sink. Plus the bathroom upstairs."

"That's okay! I can try tackling the sink if you wanna start your fight with the bathroom!" Paul once again laughs at his joke, but again I felt like he isn't actually joking.

"Are you sure? No offense but your sink is…"

"Yeah, it's okay. Besides, seeing the house this clean has me motivated!" Paul shoots me a wide smile. "Although I can't guarantee it'll look pretty, at least it gives you less work."

I give him a genuine smile. It's only been a few hours, but I can tell Paul is one of those sweet souls. A "do no harm" type of person. "Thank you, Paul. Not just for this, but for making me feel so welcomed."

"It's no problem, I appreciate having you here to help out. Looking at this house, I should be thanking you!" We both laugh together and head in different directions. He slips away to the kitchen and I head up the now spotless and clear steps.

"Okay, now for the bathroom."

I do my "dump bleach on the floor" move to try to get the floor and surfaces as clean as possible and begin to scrub away. The toilet isn't clogged, at least, but still disgusting. My arm strength is going to be amazing after this.

"Damn, I didn't know we got a maid." I whip my head around to see a tall, attractive young boy at the door. "I was wondering why it was so clean in here. I almost thought I walked into the wrong house." The boy sends a flirtatious smile towards me. I don't understand why he's showing me that type of smile while I'm cleaning pee stains off the toilet, but I'm not going to question it. He looks like the boy from the third picture, very muscular and tan; he must be an athlete.

"If you're not going in then move, I gotta go…" The boy with the dark hair pushes past his brother and steps into the bathroom. "Oh! Sorry, I didn't know…"

"Don't mind her, Charlie, she's just our new maid." He shoots me a condescending smile this time. *What a prick.*

"She's not a maid, Zach, she's the girl dad has been telling us about, the one who will be living with us for a year." The final boy appears behind Zach. "You're Michelle, right?" This boy gives me a genuine smile like Paul.

"Uh, yeah, sorry." I quickly stand up. "I'm almost done here so you can use it."

"No, it's fine, take your time." The dark-haired boy steps forward and sticks out his hand. "I'm Charlie, nice to meet you." He gives a shyer smile.

"Oh, thanks." I rip my rubber gloves off. "I would shake your hand but I've been cleaning all day so I'm probably really gross."

"You're not gross at all..." Charlie says as his eyes examine me up and down. I also take note of him. He's about as tall as Zach but not as muscular. He has more of a scrawny thin body type. He's wearing the same beanie as in his photo and has a little bit of his curly brown hair sticking out in the front.

"I don't know, she looks a little sweaty." *Prick.* I want to say that to the muscular man in front of me, but I'm a good girl who can hold her tongue. "But I'll agree you're not gross. I'm Zach." He simply nods his head at me.

"Nice to meet you both." I feel like I'm being overwhelmed in this tight space.

"Come on, guys, let her finish up in peace, we haven't seen the bathroom floor in ages." The final brother starts to push the other two out.

"Thank you...Sam, right?" Sam turns to face me, his eyes widened and cheeks flushed.

"Uh, yeah, I'm Sam, the older brother to these two goofballs."

"Yeah, older by like five minutes," Charlie adds as he's officially pushed out of the bathroom.

"We will let you finish, please take your time." Sam smiles and closes the door. At least one of them is nice, but I still don't want to judge the other two without knowing them more.

I hurry and it takes me less than ten minutes to finish up. I step out of the bathroom and only hear the TV downstairs. "Bathroom is open!" I shout down the stairs.

"That's fine, we just used the downstairs bathroom," Zach's voice shouts back.

Wait, a downstairs bathroom? Great, one more place to clean... I take a deep breath, readying myself for more work, but the creak of a door steals my attention. Sam emerges from what I assume is his room. "By downstairs bathroom, he means outside. And I think Charlie just went to the one in our dad's room so you're free to relax now."

"Oh, thank you…" I suddenly become aware of my appearance. How messy do I look for him to know I hadn't had time to relax yet?

"Oh, you look fine…really! But with how nice you were able to get this house, I assume you must have been at it for hours."

"Oh, haha, yeah, well, it gave your dad time to move my stuff upstairs."

"Have you unpacked yet? Do you need any help?"

"No, that's okay, I might take a shower first, I feel really gross."

Sam's face becomes flushed again "Oh right, yes, go right ahead." He motions towards the bathroom.

"Thank you." I nod to him silently and he just smiles and goes back to his room. I want to hit my head against the wall for how awkward I am. "Ugh, I'm such a weirdo…" I murmur under my breath.

"You're not weirder than the rest of us." I turn around to see Charlie stepping out of his room. My face goes even redder. "Sorry, I wasn't trying to eavesdrop…"

"It's fine!" I spit out and rush up to the attic, mortified by the fact he heard me. I run in and shut the door. I take a deep breath and collapse on the floor. "Well, that could have gone better…"

I try to shake off the embarrassment I just felt and finally get to look around the room. Boxes fill up the once-open space—they all look just as they did when I sent them. "I'll need to thank Paul again." I open one of my suitcases to grab my shower stuff and a clean towel. "I'll take care of this later. One step at a time, Michelle, one step at a time."

It's a great shower. After a two-hour flight, and three hours of cleaning, I needed this. As I get out of the shower and wrap my body in a towel, it dawns on me that I am naked in a house full of men. "Shit…" I'm hoping that I won't run into any of them as I open the door. "Shit." It's Zach.

He chuckles. "Don't worry, your body isn't my type." He pushes past me and shuts the door. Soon after I hear the shower water running. He really is a prick.

I quickly run up to the attic before any of the other boys pop up and put on some clean clothes. "Finally, I can start unpacking."

I carefully go through each box, grabbing my clothes first, then personal items, and lastly my $500 worth of art supplies. I'm folding up the boxes when I hear a slight knock at the door. "Yeah?"

"Hey, Michelle, it's Sam. I just wanted to let you know we're ordering a pizza tonight. Dad is trying to clean right now." I laugh to myself imagining Paul at the sink scrubbing the dishes like a madman. "Is there any kind you like?

"Uh, yeah one second… You can come in if you'd like." Knowing Sam so far, having him in my room wouldn't be a problem.

I hear a shy, "Okay," when the door opens and Sam walks in. "Whoa, that's a lot," is the first thing out of his mouth when he sees all of my art supplies. I'd set up my easel and lined my canvases along the wall. I had all of my paints in one bin on the ground next to the easel and my brushes in a bin next to the paints.

"Oh yeah, I'm a huge art fan, it's my goal in life to have my pieces hung in a famous museum."

"Wow, do you have any of your paintings here?"

"No, I tend to not keep my pieces after I'm finished. I usually sell or donate them, but I do have pictures of them on my phone if you wanna see them."

"Yeah sure, I would love to." I hand my phone over to Sam and see his face light up with each picture he scrolls by. "I hear that you're very talented, too. You made all the furniture in my room."

Sam looks up at me with red cheeks. "Oh, so he told you? I was hoping to keep it a secret."

I laugh lightly. "Why? You should be proud of your art."

"Yeah, but I guess I have a confidence problem. My dad loves my work, my friends and teachers love my work, but I always feel I'm lacking." Sam looks down to avoid my eye contact.

"I get that. There have been many pieces of mine that I just threw out because I hated them so much!"

Sam lets out a laugh. "Same! I swear I almost smashed that dresser to pieces about a million times, my dad had to hold me back."

"Really? Well, I'm glad he did, the dresser is beautiful." I didn't realize how comfortable I'd be talking to Sam. Sam looks shy at the compliment. "I can see you don't take compliments well."

"Yeah…I guess that I…"

"Damn, you unpacked fast. And here I was hoping I could be the hero and help you out." Oh great, this guy.

Zach stands at the open door in just a towel. Long hair sticks to his neck and drips water on the ground. With his shirt off I can clearly see how muscular he is. A full six-pack with no hair in sight. It's like he's trying to show off.

"Thanks for the thought but I don't need your help." I try to let my annoyance be known through my voice.

"Well, it's a nice setup you have." Zach waltzes right into my room and starts walking around. He picks up a photo I had put on my nightstand. "Is this a family photo?"

I rush over and grab the frame out of his hand. "It's just me and my mom."

"You look a lot like her." He says this in a soft voice, like he's trying to come off as a down-to-earth friendly guy, as if he isn't standing in my room with only a towel on.

"Hey, no one told me there was a party happening up here?" Charlie pokes his head into my room. For the first time I see him without his beanie on, and his head just has soft dark brown curls around it.

"It's not a party, you guys, I was just asking Michelle what type of pizza she wants," Sam states, clearly annoyed with his brothers barging in.

"Oh, I'll take plain!" Charlie says, as he comes further into my room.

"I'll have pepperoni," Zach adds, but his eyes are on me the entire time.

"Okay okay…" Sam looks at me and speaks with a gentle voice again. "What about you, Michelle?"

"I also like plain."

"So you and I share similar tastes," Charlie says with a smile on his face. He's found his way onto my bed somehow.

"Having similar taste in pizza doesn't mean anything." Zach immediately goes into defensive mode. "The majority of people like plain. Also, off her bed." Zach grabs Charlie's arm to pull him off.

"At least I'm not naked in her room." Charlie rips his arm out of Zach's grasp.

"What? I bet she likes it." Zach winks at me. "Most girls do."

I can't hold back my disgust. "Yeah, you are *not* my type." I try to enunciate the "not."

Zach's face drops a little bit.

"Ooooh, first time being rejected?" Charlie seems to enjoy rubbing it in his face. He finally gets up and walks over to me. "I get it, you're more into the sensitive type, right?" He smiles, probably talking about himself.

"Yeah, you're not my type either." My face probably has a look of disgust on it at this point.

Zach bursts out into a laugh. "Well, Charlie, looks like we both lost out. I guess Sam is the lucky one." The way the words come out of his mouth sound like a joke but give off a frustrated feeling. "We should leave the two lovebirds alone." Zach smiles and disappears after that.

Both Sam and I try to say something but Zach has already dragged Charlie out and slammed the door. It's now quiet but awkward.

Sam speaks up first. "Sorry about those two. I guess they got excited about having a pretty girl here." Sam's face goes red with the realization he called me pretty. "Wait, I mean…"

"It's okay," I interrupt Sam. I honestly want to change the topic. "Those two are quite the characters."

Sam laughs lightly "Haha yeah… You have no idea…"

Silence.

"I should go order those pizzas now. Sorry about all of this."

"You know what, it made my first night here exciting!" I try to laugh off everything to reassure Sam since he seems concerned.

"Then I'm glad." He walks towards the door. "I'll call you down when it's here."

"Thanks." And with that, Sam is out of the room and I am finally by myself.

"Ahhh." I plop down on my bed. "What am I going to do?" Looks like I'll be living with two wild boys, one nice one, and a kind father. Will I be able to survive this year?

Chapter 2

BEEP. BEEP. BEEP. BEEP. BE—

I slam my hand down on the alarm. It's morning and my first day at a new school. It's still too dark out for me to see any sun shining through my window, so I make my way stumbling through the dark looking for my light switch.

"Aaaaahn," I let a long yawn slip from my mouth as I stretch my arms up. "Okay, Michelle, let's do this." I lightly slap my cheeks to wake myself up more before moving on.

My outfit for the first day is the style I usually wear. A nice modest dress. Most people at my school in Philly wore chic clothes as a fashion statement, but I was okay with a simple dress that would hang below my knees. I would call myself a dressy dresser. I throw on a light white short-sleeved T-shirt and the dress after. It's a spaghetti-strapped blue dress that goes down to my ankles. I climb into a pair of white socks and black flats to match and there, a typical Michelle look.

As I begin to head down from the attic I can hear shuffling and groaning from downstairs. When I reach the second floor I run into a still pajama-wearing Charlie. His pajamas are what I expected. A black T-shirt and gray boxers.

"Ahhh, morning." Charlie yawns at me.

"Morning…" Before I can fully respond he disappears into his room. "Okay then…" I make my way to the bathroom to wash my face and brush my teeth.

The door swings open. "Damn, you clean up nice." *Great, this guy.* I turn to see a once-again shirtless Zach.

"I'm starting to think you don't own any shirts."

For some reason, he laughs at my comment. "I'm just not used to having a girl in the house. I'll make sure to put on more clothes if you're uncomfortable."

"Thanks." I spit into the sink.

"Anyway, don't take too long with your makeup, I gotta go."

"I'm actually all done so you're free to use." I try to squeeze by him in peace but of course, he has to respond.

"So, you're one of those girls who doesn't believe in makeup? Think that all girls who wear makeup are trashy?"

I honestly don't want to respond to him but his comment irritates me. "Actually, I like makeup quite a lot. As an artist, I appreciate makeup and how people use it to express themselves. I personally don't put on makeup in the morning because I'm too tired and too lazy." I once again turn to leave but of course…

"Huh… Well, I like that. You're quite different, you know."

"If you try to say I'm not like other girls I will punch you in the face."

As I hear Zach laugh, I quickly exit before he can say more and head down to the kitchen. The smell of toast and bacon fill the air.

"Morning, Michelle! I'm glad you made it down for breakfast!" Paul stands at the now-clean stove frying up some scrambled eggs.

Seeing Paul I am immediately reminded I left him to clean the sink and dishes by himself. My eyes travel to the sink which is…relatively clean. There are still some dried stains and food on the faucet but the pile of dishes and rotting food is gone.

"I'm sorry for leaving you to clean the sink and dishes all by yourself. It must have taken a while."

"It's okay, Sam ended up helping me out."

"What did I do?" A well-dressed Sam enters the kitchen. His outfit mirrors his friendly nature. He sports a vibrant, sky-blue hoodie with a comfy white T-shirt peeking out. His pair of worn-in denim jeans tells volumes about his laid-back attitude.

"I was just telling her about how you helped me with the dishes."

"Oh, it was no big deal, If I didn't help you out, you would still be cleaning."

A light laugh slips from my mouth. The image of coming downstairs and seeing Paul still cleaning the sink makes me giggle, unable to contain my amusement at the idea of Paul's dedication to making the sink spotless.

Sam turns his attention to me. "Did you have a good night?"

"Yeah, it was fine, I'm just nervous about the new school. I've never really been good at making friends."

"Well, you have the two of us…"

"Two?"

"Me and Charlie will be your friends and there to support you."

A knowing smile creeps onto my lips. "And what about Zach?"

"Yeah… He's… Well, the less said the better but you have me."

I can't help but smile at Sam's kindness.

"You guys talking shit about me?" Charlie rolls up in a black T-shirt with another band logo I don't recognize on it, ripped-up faded jeans, and of course, a black beanie.

"Sam was just saying that if I have trouble making friends you'll be there for me."

I don't know what I was expecting but Charlie's eyes widen in astonishment, a mixture of surprise and delight illuminating his face. A bashful yet hopeful smile slowly spreads across his lips. "Yeah, I'll be there for you, no matter what."

"Can I get that in writing?" I say with a laugh. He laughs, too, but I'm not quite sure he understands my joke.

"Come on, everyone, come sit and eat." Paul rushes through us with a pan of crackling bacon he just pulled from the oven. "Sam, grab the eggs and toast!"

Sam sighs. His head drops and shoulders slump, burdened by the endless tasks they've shouldered for so long. As he goes to grab the plates of food, slight frustration flickers in his eyes. Charlie doesn't even bat an eye and waltzes right into the dining room.

"Here let me help." I take the plate of unevenly stacked toast and walk away before he can protest. As an only child, I understand taking on all of the household responsibilities, but I can't imagine how it must feel when there are two other people, but you are the one tasked with everything.

We place the food down on the table and out of thin air Zach's hand appears over the plate and snags a piece.

"Thanks for the food." He gobbles the toast, leaving crumbs scattered like a confetti explosion. The rest of the family grabs at the food like they haven't had a meal in years. They look like mice scurrying for the last drop. There's plenty of food so I'm not sure what the rush is.

"Here, this is for you." Sam places a plate of scrambled eggs, three pieces of bacon, and a piece of toast in front of me.

"I could have gotten it myself." But when I look towards the center of the table, all the food is gone. Most of it ended up on Zach's plate, but Paul also has a great deal. All Charlie is left with is bacon crumbs.

"Zach here likes to eat a lot, so we try to grab as much food as we can before he takes it all."

"'M 'an a'lete, gotta eat awot," Zach says as he munches away.

"Hey, don't talk with food in your mouth!" Paul says, while shoveling food into his mouth.

"Ugh, Zach's on the football team so he feels entitled to take all of our food."

Zach swallows enough to spit out, "Fuck off, Charlie." Charlie presents him with a middle finger in return. So I was right to assume that Zach is an athlete. It also explains the white and blue football jersey he has on.

I turn to Sam, my only solace. "Is this how mornings usually go for you guys?"

He gives me a pitiful look. "Yeah, hopefully you'll get used to it."

With the gladiator fight known as breakfast over, the boys go upstairs to finish getting ready, which basically meant covering themselves with enough body spray to destroy the rainforest. I stay downstairs to clean up.

"Wow, it's like watching a magician make a rabbit appear from this hat." Paul looks in awe at the wiped-down counters and hand-washed pans.

"It's much easier to clean when there is a smaller amount. Thank you for taking care of the dishes…really."

"It's no problem at all." Paul smiles with joy in his eyes, but his eyes take a sharp turn and become focused. "I need to leave for work now, so I won't be able to see you off. The boys share one car so you will all drive to and leave school together. Sometimes Zach has to stay til dark for late night football practice and will catch a ride home with a friend, so on those days it'll just be Sam and Charlie in the car." *Those days will probably be my favorite.* "Here's three-hundred dollars for the work you did yesterday." Paul hands me a wad of fifties and twenties.

"Wait, hold on, this is way too much!" I try to push the cash back to him but he closes my hand around the bills and with a double tap on the back of my hand, he reassures me that the money is mine.

"Spend it wisely." A quick wink and Paul grabs his keys and is out the door.

"Welp At least I have some spending money now." I'm at a crossroads feeling guilty for taking so much money, but at the same time appreciating being rewarded for the hard work. I make sure that all of the bills make it safely into my wallet by carefully nuzzling them into an open slot. "I promise to spend it wisely."

"Spend what wisely?"

I jump and spin to face that annoying, irritating voice I've gotten to know. "Jesus, Zach, are you a ninja or something?"

He throws his head back in a deep-throated laugh. "I don't know, should I be one?" His response gets a slight giggle out of me, but my hand shoots up to my mouth, hoping he doesn't notice. "Hey, I saw that, I actually made you laugh." A smile beams across his face like a kid who was told he was getting a puppy.

"Oh please, one small giggle shouldn't count as a triumph. Also I was only laughing at how stupid you are."

"Yeah, sure you were." He can't hold back his condescending tone as he steps towards me, slowly closing the gap between us. My muscles tense up as my feet stumble back bit by bit, until...

"Hey!" my savior, Sam, calls out from the staircase. My chest and muscles begin to relax as Zach moves back. "We're going to be late." Sam speaks as if to say, "Stop it, you're scaring the poor girl."

"Alright, alright, fine...CHARLIE!"

"I'M COMING, JEEZ!" I can feel Charlie's stomping feet from above. I track them as he leaves his room, goes down the hall, and appears on the stairs. "Let's go."

Zach heads out first with Charlie following behind. As Sam walks by me he gives me a look that says, "You okay?" I nod in return.

The boys drive a sleek blue Ford Mustang. It gives a stylish yet aggressive appearance. It's exactly what I'd imagined they would drive, something dynamic and sporty. Sam naturally slips into the driver's side and I take a back seat to be considerate. What I don't expect is Zach and Charlie pushing and shoving each other to get in the back seat as well.

"Why don't you go to the front seat, haven't you always complained about sitting in the back?" Zach says through his teeth, as his shoulder digs into Charlie's frail body.

"But I thought you liked sitting up front, that's why you always take that spot." Charlie's teeth clench as he fights to barely push Zach back.

"Fine, if none of you want to sit up front I will. Besides, I get carsick in the back." Getting out of the car, I walk by the stunned bodies of Zach and Charlie and sit myself beside Sam. With a winning smile, he sits up and turns the car on. I look back at the still-frozen Zach and Charlie, their mouths agape as if they want to say something. "Satisfied?"

The laugh starts quietly as if Sam is trying to conceal it, but as Charlie and Zach's defeated bodies slump into the back seat, he can't keep it down. Sam's eyes appear in the rearview mirror. "Make sure you guys buckle up," he says between laughs and with that, we're on the road.

We drive in the opposite direction from the way I came in with Paul so I'm able to see a different side of the town. There *is* a town. Just very small. No tall skyscrapers or rows of restaurants but more of a shopping strip with a nail/hair salon, a clothing store, an electronic store, and a pharmacy. Across from it is a large restaurant/bar, probably the biggest restaurant for a while. Most of the other places to eat are smaller shops attached to each other. In the center of the town is a large church with a small police station poking out from behind it. That's basically the closest town to me.

As we drive through, Sam points everything out to me, although it doesn't take long. He tells me there's another, larger, town an hour away. I'm not so confident about how large this other town may be, but apparently, there's at least a movie theater and shopping mall.

We drive through the small town and past a couple of neighborhoods before the moderate-sized school appears in my line of view. My eyes widen at the sight of the school nestled in the far corner of the town. Its faded red brick walls bear marks of countless generations but exclude any sense of history or charm. Teenagers loiter all around the parking lot and entrance. Some are sitting on top of their cars and chatting away, while others are hunched over hastily writing things into their notebooks. I watch as friends run to greet each other after the summer break, lovers share a sweet kiss, and the nerdy kids run by fast in the hope of not being spotted. We pull into an open parking spot as kids ride their bikes past us, some even on skateboards.

"Do you guys have school buses?" I turn to Sam, who's preparing himself to face the school day.

"Yeah, the school buses even drive out to our neighborhood to pick up kids, but you have to be ready at five a.m. to catch it, it sucks. But it was the only option for most of us."

Charlie adds, "Sometimes our mom would drive us if it was snowing or we were too tired to wake up."

I don't know how to respond to Charlie mentioning their mom so I just nod with an, "Oh."

"Yep. Anyway. I'm glad we have a car." Charlie kicks open the door and stretches, Zach already long out of the car and talking to the group I saw by the cars earlier. I'm surprised to see his arm around a girl in the group, and even more surprised that she's cuddling him back.

I cautiously open the door, stepping out into the great unknown, that being the middle of nowhere Ohio. Charlie comes up from behind me and swings his arm over my shoulder, guiding me to my next destination.

"Don't worry, new girl, we'll make sure no one harms you."

I push myself away from him. "Yeah, I don't need help with that...I just..." I hesitate, not sure if I can truly rely on these boys yet.

"Just what?" But seeing Sam's warm and assuring smile tells me I can.

"I just...don't want to be a loner again."

Sam and Charlie exchange a look, but I don't dare see what kind of faces they're making.

"Well." Charlie matches his steps with mine. "You can't be a loner this year since you have us following you around."

Sam follows suit. "That's right, even if you try, you're not getting rid of us."

"Yeah, literally, you live with us now, so…" Charlie pulls me into a tight bear hug, lifting my feet off the ground. "We're not ever letting you go!"

"Okay, okay! But let me go now I can't breathe!" I say through the genuine smile that has formed on my lips. I walk ahead to turn and face them. "Thank you, guys…really."

Charlie's face blushes with a shy smile, attempting to appear casual but unable to contain joy inside. "It's nothing really…"

Sam's eyes light up with sparks and with a gentle tone of warmth in his voice says, "Anytime."

Our newly formed friendship embarks on our senior year.

Chapter 3

"So, what's your first class?" Charlie's walking unnaturally close to me, his shoulder constantly brushing up against mine, his feet chasing mine like a cold catching his shadow.

I look over my schedule. "Ugh, pre-calc, I hate math."

"Oh, I have pre-calc, too! With Mr. Greene, right?" Sam's bright eyes scan my schedule.

"Umm, no mine says I have Mrs. McConnell."

"Oh, yeah, I take AP classes…just for the higher GPA." Sam's eyes look away from me as if he feels ashamed to be taking a higher-level course just for grades.

"Yeah well, one, I hate math, and two, I don't take AP classes since I don't even care about grades or GPA… I don't even really want to go to college…"

The boys on my sides stop, but only for a moment, so short you wouldn't have noticed unless you were paying attention…but I was paying attention.

"Oh…cool, I respect that," Charlie says nonchalantly.

"Do you mind if I ask why? If it's not hard to talk about."

Sam is just too pure for this world. "No, it's okay. It's not a sob story or anything. I just want to be an artist…and you don't *need* to go to an art school to be a professional artist. I mean like, some do, but I'm more self-taught."

"Oh, yeah I can understand that. I mean, your art is really good."

"Like I said I respect that…but wait, did you say her art is good? Did Sam get to see your art and not me?" Charlie's arm movements begin to get more frantic. "No fair! I want to see her art!"

Before any of us can respond the bell goes off and we're pushed apart as bodies rush from class to class. Sam, Charlie, and I get separated in the chaos. My breath quickens with my heart pounding against my chest. I feel as though the walls are closing in on me. Where am I going? Who can I ask? Where's Sam and Charlie?

As more students rush towards me, I fall back into the muscular arms of some stranger. Except it isn't a stranger.

"Zach?"

He looks down, a smile on his face. "Let's get you to Mrs. McConnell's class." He grabs my hand and leads me down the once bustling hallway, the crowd now parted for us. As we walk by I can feel stares and hear whispers around me. The quick heavy breathing returns. I'm not someone who is fond of this kind of attention. I'd be much happier disappearing into the masses.

I need to distract myself. "How did you know about my classes?"

"Simple, I took a look at your schedule." Zach doesn't even look at me, he just keeps marching forward.

"Stalker."

"Just wanted to make sure you would be alright on your first day, newbie."

I roll my eyes. "Please, I would have been fine." We stop in front of a door with "McConnell" on a plaque next to it.

"Sure you would." He leans close to my ear. "That's why you looked like you were about to cry."

I jump back. "I was *not*!" But with a slick smile and a wink, he's off. *God, he's so infuriating!*

I calm myself, take deep breaths, walk into the classroom, and land in the first empty seat I find. I try not to look around but I can still feel the eyes on me. Their stares burn holes in my back. I slump down into my chair. *I guess I'll be a loner again.*

"Hi there! I'm Chloe!" I wait for a second before turning my head towards the voice. I was waiting to see if someone else would respond but they didn't. I turn to see a pale burgundy headed girl inches from my face.

Startled, I recoil. "Whoa…hi…"

The red-headed girl giggles softly and leans back in her chair, her piercing blue eyes fixated on me. "Sorry! Didn't mean to scare you. I'm just excited to meet you!"

"Excited to meet me?" I answer with a bit of annoyance in my voice. "Why are you excited to meet me? I literally just got here." The girl's eyes soften a bit and raise slightly. *Shit.* My response sounded more snarky than I meant it to. Just when I decided to work on that. "Sorry, that was rude of me. Umm, I'm Michelle, and you're Chloe?"

"Yeah! And don't worry about it, I was being way forward, a lot of people say I don't have a filter sometimes."

"That's okay, people tell me I can be a snarky asshole sometimes." As we both laugh, I start to relax around her.

"And the reason I was excited to meet you was because *you* are the girl!" My confusion must be plastered all over my face. "So, we heard about a girl moving in with the Owens', and we were all curious about who the lucky girl was—like what type of girl she was, if she was pretty, and you know, all those things."

"Oh wow…didn't know I was already a celebrity." I'm unimpressed that people are curious about me, it annoys me more than anything.

"Well. The Owens triplets are basically celebrities and thus, anyone associated with them is too."

I laugh to myself. "They're celebrities?"

"Omg yes!" Before Chloe can explode into words the teacher walks in.

"Okay, class, let's begin the new year off with a good start."

The teacher starts her speech about how we're seniors now and blah blah blah.

"Psst." Chloe leans closer to me with a hand covering her mouth. "Walk with me after class and I'll give you the rundown."

I give her a slight nod. An excited chill runs up my spine as my heart beats a little faster. Could this be a new friend?

The class goes by in a flash. It's hard to pay attention in a class you don't care about. I sluggishly rise from my seat when Chloe's arm links with mine and pulls me through the hallways.

"Okay, so basically the Owens triplets are royalty here, all the girls are in love with them." Chloe goes on as she drags me through the once-again bustling halls, pushing through clumps of students. "Sam's the sensitive green flag type; some girls have confessed their feelings to him, but he's never dated—by the way, what's your next class?" Before I can read my schedule Chloe grabs it out of my hand. "Okay cool, so we have all of our classes together, except electives."

She drags me into our next classroom and sits us down next to each other. Her voice hushed to a whisper, she says, "Girls have a game where they go and ask Sam out. They know he'll most likely say no, but it's like our school's version of pulling the sword out of the stone, you know?"

"I don't know…"

"It's like, girls know he won't say yes, but it's exciting to think, 'What if I'm the special one?'" I nod but don't quite understand. Still, having Chloe rant to me is making class go by faster.

Like clockwork, the bell rings and Chloe is dragging me around again. "Charlie…he's so hot. He's the mysterious and cool one. He listens to a bunch of indie bands and plays a little guitar on the side."

"Really? I haven't heard him play or anything."

"He's in a local band, I think they practice at one of the other member's houses. Oh, this is the art room, you have your next class here. Meet me at lunch, okay?" She gives a thumbs-up and runs off.

I just stand there, taking in the major information dump. "That was…a lot." I turn to face the art room. The two electives I picked were painting and ceramics. "Hello, my new home for the next year." I swing the door open with confidence.

The room is jam-packed with art supplies and products. Shelves are coated with layers of dried paint, crushed-up paint bottles are smushed together to try to fit on the shelves. Brushes lay around the room, most having a colored tint on the tips from dried paint. Drawers are popping out, overflowing with all sorts of materials: rulers, glitter, clay, markers, googly eyes, and so on. The only thing that isn't packed is the seats.

About six other students sit apart from each other at different corners of the room. Most of them are sketching in a book while one of the girls is behind an easel. I take a slow scan of the whole room and see a small desk with a teacher barely peeking out behind piles of papers.

I make my way to her desk, tiptoeing to not alarm the other students.

"Umm, excuse me," I squeak in a low tone.

The teacher's eyes pop up over the pile. "Are you Michelle?"

"Yes."

"I'm Ms. Park. This is an advanced class, so you have free range over anything in this room. You have an hour to work on anything you want. Have fun." Her eyes once again vanish behind the mountain of papers.

"Okay." I sneak around to an open easel. I take a deep breath. Probably the first breath I really take today. I pick up a pencil to start sketching something when the unseen person next to me pokes out her head.

"Psst!" Her blue hair catches my eye at first. "You're Michelle, right?" I can clearly see the girl who was hiding behind the easel. Her whole body is like a canvas. Her natural curls are dyed a vibrant neon blue, which match her blue eyeshadow and lipstick which pop out against her dark skin. Her pants look like they're made from different types of fabric sewn together.

"Umm, yeah, I'm Michelle, are you one of my many fans?"

A smile creeps onto her mouth as she lets out a little laugh. "You're a funny one, aren't you?"

"I'm a little cheeky."

"I'm Chloe's friend, she's been texting me about you all day. I'm Sasha." Sasha reaches out her hand to mine.

I take her hand. "I hope she's been saying good things."

"Oh yeah, look at the last text she sent me."

Sasha shows me her phone. *hey girlie!! Just dropped her off at the art classroom. I leave her to you, please protect her!*

I can't help but smile. *She's worried about me?*

"Anyway, if you have any questions regarding the school and you know, *not* about the Owens triplets, let me know."

We laugh together; I guess she knows Chloe well.

"Is there an art club? How do I join?"

"Oh yeah, there's a club. I'm in it, just come here after the bell rings, it's literally just this." She motions around her.

"Are all of the art classes like this?"

"No, just the advanced classes. Ms. Park uses this class to grade papers and other things."

"Yeah, that makes sense."

Sasha answers all of the questions I have. About the school system, teachers I should avoid, etc. At least I get a whole hour without hearing about the Owens triplets.

As the bell rings, we head out together. "Chloe asked me to bring you to lunch to sit with us."

"Oh cool…I get to hear more about the famous triplets." I emphasize "famous." I think the whole thing is bullshit; they're just high school boys, and they're not a big deal.

"Yeah, sorry about that. She means well, but she's had a major crush on one of them since middle school. It's super obvious so you'll find out soon."

"Oh…" I feel a pinch in my heart. The thought that she only befriended me to get close to her secret crush hurts a little.

"I'm not interested in any of them though…and Chloe isn't like that. From what she has said, she seems to like you."

"Cool." I nod but I don't believe it...I think Sasha is able to pick up on that, but she doesn't say anything.

We step into the buzzing cafeteria, students moving around like rushing bees. Chloe's body shoots up and she starts waving her hand frantically. We walk over and put our bags down at the table.

"Oh my god! So Michelle, about Zach..."

Sasha puts her hand up, stopping Chloe. "Please let the girl eat, and then you can go on a rant."

"Right, sorry." Chloe's body slinks down on the bench.

"Come on, let's go." Sasha leads me through the lunch line. I notice fewer people staring at me, but there are a few people shooting daggers at me with their eyes.

Walking back to the table I was almost safe but...

"Hey." Zach's large body appears next to mine.

Oh great. People start to stare again. "What?" I utter in a low tone.

"Thought I'd help you out again, I got a seat for you at my table." He tries taking my tray.

I pull it away from him, unimpressed. "No thanks, I'm going to sit with my new friends." I begin walking toward Chloe without looking back. I hear the sound of "ooOoo!" coming from the students around but I don't care.

When I sit down, I see Zach going to his table. His friends wearing matching football jerseys push him around while laughing. The blonde girl to his left hits him on the shoulder. *What an ass...*

"I can't believe you just did that!" Chloe said, her face a little too close to mine.

"Did what?"

"Reject Zach? No one rejects Zach!"

I shrug "I just did… what's the big deal?"

Chloe beams "Can I tell you about Zach now?"

I take a deep breath, preparing myself. "Sure, go ahead."

Chloe leans in. "Okay so, as you can probably tell, Zach is the ladies man of our school. While Sam dates none of his admirers, Zach dates all of them. Well, I should say 'dates.' The longest relationship he's had is like two weeks. Except for Maddy." Chloe nods her head towards the table. "The girl sitting next to him, they've been on and off since eighth grade. They'll be together, break up, he 'dates' another girl, and then two weeks later they get back together."

"Damn, sounds like a lot of work."

"Yeah, but you have to admit he's attractive, right?"

"Meh…" I rock my hand back and forth to show my indifference.

"That's okay, I don't find him attractive either," Sasha adds while shoving a fry in her mouth.

"Yeah, you totally didn't have a crush on him in sixth grade," Chloe emphasizes.

Sasha's cheeks flush with color "That was eight years ago! I've matured."

"Yeah yeah, anyway." Chloe directs her focus to me. "If you don't find Zach attractive then maybe Sam…or Charlie?" Chloe hesitates before saying Charlie's name. She even looks upset when she says it. *Ah, so it's Charlie.*

"Why do I need to find any of them attractive?"

Chloe reacts as if I've just told her the tooth fairy doesn't exist. "I mean, you get to live with them for a year! Surely some romance will develop! It's like the perfect plot for a movie!"

I sigh. *Guess I have to tell the truth.* "Umm actually…I'm a lesbian."

Chapter 4

"A…what?" Chloe says, her face contorting as she tries to understand what I just said.

"Yeah, lesbian…it means I like girls."

The two girls exchange looks as Chloe sits back and Sasha scoots away from me.

I roll my eyes. "Don't worry, I'm not interested in any of you. Also," I begin to go off on a rant, "it can come off as homophobic to assume every lesbian girl is into *every* girl. I mean, you're not into every boy, right?" I'm disappointed. I knew it would be like this, it's always like this. Every time, after I would tell my friends that I liked girls, they would assume I liked them and stop talking to me, leaving me alone. I don't know why I thought this time would be different.

I'm preparing myself to move to a different seat when Chloe speaks up. "So, I guess I should be asking if there are any girls you like?" Her gaze is hesitant at first, waiting for my response.

Sasha moves closer to me. "Sorry, we just…we've never actually met a lesbian before. I mean, not in this town."

"Yeah, we weren't trying to be disrespectful or homophobic or anything! We just, we're just surprised and…" Chloe runs her fingers through her hair in distress. "I'm sorry."

I try to keep it in at first, but I can't hold back, my laughter begins to spill out like a cascade of joy. The two girls look at me in confusion.

"I'm sorry, just seeing you guys get so worked up over this. It's not that big of a deal."

"Really?" Chloe's eyes blink, trying to process.

"Well, it is a big deal, but you don't need to beat yourself up over it. Most people just tell me I'm gross and move on with life. No one's ever tried to apologize."

"They tell you you're gross? And you're just fine with that?" Chloe looks as though I slapped her. I'm taken aback by how angry she's getting on my behalf.

"I mean, it sucks, but I'm used to it at this point." The girls exchange concerned looks. "It's fine, really, I know who I am and I'm not ashamed of it. If other people have an issue with me being gay that's their problem. I don't need that type of person in my life."

To my surprise, Sasha puts her hand on mine. "Just so you know, I don't have any issues with it."

"Okay." I'm not sure how to respond—this is the first time I've gotten a positive reaction, and I'm caught off guard.

"Me too! I don't have any problems with you being…" Chloe hushes to a whisper. "A lesbian."

I let out a hardy laugh. "You guys don't have to be all secretive about it. I'm not trying to hide it or anything, but if no one asks I'm not going to tell them."

"Oh, sorry." Chloe's cheeks turn pink as she hides her face.

"Please don't apologize. Like I said it's not that big of a deal, but thanks for not calling me gross. This is actually the first time people have been okay with me after I tell them I'm gay." I'm in shock at their response. I'm so used to being exiled that the idea of people being okay with me was nonexistent.

"Of course! I'm super chill about it." Chloe leans her head on her hand to make a "cool" pose.

"You're the least chill person I know… and I've known you for fourteen years," says Sasha.

"Okay, Miss I-Used-to-Write-Mrs.-Zach-Owens-in-Her-Notebook."

"That was in *sixth grade*!"

"Anyway…" Chloe diverts her attention to me again. "Are there any girls you like?"

"Umm, not that I've seen."

"Hey, you found a seat without us!" I feel an arm swing around my shoulder and Charlie plops down next to me. Sam sits across from me, next to Chloe.

"Yeah, I'm…I'm sitting with my friends." I smile at Chloe and Sasha, hoping they won't correct me.

"Yeah, that's right. We are her friends," Sasha says as she brushes off Charlie's arm and pulls me closer to her.

"Yeah, we have almost every class together so we will be besties in no time." Chloe speaks much faster than she has been. I see her face blushing and her eyes peeking at Charlie. *Oh, it's totally Charlie.*

The rest of the day goes by in a blur. Sam and Charlie join us for an awkward lunch. Afterward, everyone decides to walk me to my next class. I don't know why they're treating me like I don't know how to walk.

In my classes with Chloe, she tries asking about girls I've liked but I get her off on a tangent by asking about Charlie.

"Oh my god! How did you know?"

"You made it really obvious."

Soon school's over, and it's time to head to clubs. Chloe and I meet up with Sasha so we can walk to art club together.

"Chloe, are you in any clubs?"

"I'm in the go-home club!" No one laughs. "I didn't want to join any clubs."

"Well, I can't leave school until pretty boy Zach is done with football practice. So all three of us…you know, me, Sam, and *Charlie*…" I take a dramatic pause for effect. "We all have to join clubs."

"But Charlie's not in a club! I would have known!" Sasha and I go silent again.

"Chlo, your stalker side is showing again."

"So what does Charlie do after school…?" I ask.

"Well, knowing him as his *stalker*"—she makes it a point to look at Sasha—"probably band pra…" Chloe's eyes go to the end of the hallway. Her mouth hangs open. "Uh oh…"

Sasha turns to look. "Crap, major bitch alert…we should go." Sasha starts leading my arm away but I turn to see what they're looking at.

A tall, blond, beautiful girl walks towards us. Her long wavy hair resembles a mermaid, and her dark blue eyes make me think of the deep ocean. She has long legs, made to look longer due to the pale blue skinny jeans she's wearing. Her thin white lace blouse bounces with each step she takes in her heels.

"Who is that?"

"Zach's on-again-off-again girlfriend, Maddy, the one who was sitting at his table. She can be a real bitch sometimes, especially to those she thinks Zach is into." Chloe tries to pull me away, but I stand my ground facing the beautiful girl.

"So, you're the Owens's new little maid?"

"Yeah."

"Well I just want you to know that Zach's only being nice to you to sleep with you..."

"Uh-huh."

"You're not special or anything...you're just one of many girls..."

"Of course."

"So don't even bother getting close to him. He would never go for a plain chore girl like you! Got it?"

I barely hear what she's saying. I'm too busy studying her features. The way she does her makeup. The perfect line she gets with her liner. How she uses soft colors as her eye shadow and puts a touch of shimmer at the corner of her eyes. She's waiting for me to reply. But the only thing I can muster up is, "You're beautiful."

Her eyes widen as she stumbles backward, caught off guard by my response. Her already rosy cheeks get redder.

She scoffs, "Excuse me?" She's flustered as she tries to come up with something to say. "Don't think I'll let you off the hook just because of a simple compliment, okay? I have my eyes on you, new girl!" She storms off, her heels clicking through the emptied halls.

My eyes don't leave her as she walks off. I'm too stunned to speak, my heartbeat began speeding up and my knees beginning to buckle.

"I think I'm in love."

Chloe and Sasha appear on both sides of me.

"Really? Head Girl Maddy?" Sasha can't hide her confusion.

"She's the most beautiful girl I've ever seen."

"Yeah, and she's the meanest girl you'll ever meet!" Chloe adds.

"Please, I've dealt with worse."

Chloe steps in front of me. "Girlie, she's tormented almost half of the girls at this school! And not just verbally! She dumped all of Sharen Lubinski's belongings into a muddy puddle."

"Yeah, one time she even stuck out her leg to trip someone and she fell down the stairs! She had to walk on crutches for a month!"

"She'll 'accidentally' bump into you in the lunchroom and make you spill all of your lunch."

"She'll spread a rumor that you slept with your cousin!"

Chloe whispers into Sasha's ear, "Actually, I heard that one was true." Sasha's eyes go wide and her mouth shuts.

As the girls go back and forth I notice something. "But it sounds like she's only doing these things to girls?"

Chloe shouts in excitement, "Yes! She's a menace to all girls!"

I think for a bit; something doesn't seem right with me. "Yeah, but do you think maybe she's being this way because of how many times Zach's cheated on her?" As I think about it, the more it makes sense and I start to sympathize with her. "She's become afraid of other girls since she knows Zach will go after them...so she probably tries to chase them away first." As I say this and the realization comes to me, I go from feeling sad for Maddy to ticked off at Zach.

Chloe looks in thought for a while. "I guess, but she harassed Sasha for no reason!"

I turn to Sasha who is looking away. "Yeah, she would steal my books. I got in a lot of trouble for not returning library books. But I mean, that was like four years ago." Sasha is trying to play it off as no big deal but I can tell she's still hurting inside.

"She was...probably jealous of how pretty you look. And I'm saying that in a platonic way, just so you know." My plan works as the girls giggle and the awkward tension lessens. I need to change the subject. "Anyway, we'll be late for club so let's get going."

I want to get away from the situation before I make things worse. Besides, I feel more comfortable being at an easel with a paintbrush. Chloe waves and heads out, as Sasha and I head upstairs to the art room.

I feel bad about digging up some bad memories, and I don't want to lose my new friends. Especially since Sasha was so nice to me all day.

"Sorry about...bringing up some things from the past."

"It's okay, it was a while ago, I've gotten over it..." I can see in her eyes it doesn't seem to bother her much, but still...

"Even if you did...being bullied like that isn't easy for anyone..." *I would know.*

"Yeah, but what you said about Maddy...you're not wrong." Sasha begins reminiscing. "She used to be really sweet, a friend to everyone, but after she started dating Zach...she changed."

So, as I thought, Zach is the issue. I need to find out more about my goddess. "What kind of change?"

"Well, she used to be someone who would be friends with anyone, no matter who they were. If she saw someone was sitting alone she would invite them to sit with her. She would also invite the whole class to her parties. She was just...super chill. But then she started dating Zach."

I hold my breath and focus on Sasha, listening to every last word.

"She stopped hanging out with other people, she just hung out with Zach's friends and the cheerleaders. She didn't invite anyone to her parties, and then she started the bullying."

"I'm sorry that that happened to you."

"Like I said, it was a while ago."

"But still…"

Sasha grabs my arm and drags me up the stairs. "Come on, we're going to be late, I don't want anyone taking my seat."

As we rush up, I get nervous thinking the room will be packed and I won't have room to create. As we push open the doors, we walk into three other people.

"You lied to me."

"Sorry! Still, let's not think about the past." Sasha walks off to sit at the same easel she had during class. I wander over to the messy shelves of art supplies.

"You have two of my classes." I turn to see Ms. Park standing behind me. She's a tall thin woman who looks to be about thirty. She doesn't look like a typical art teacher. She's wearing a plain black turtleneck with a gray pencil skirt. Her long black hair is slicked back into a ponytail and you can see dark circles under her glasses. You would expect an art teacher to have crazy hair and colorful clothes, but Ms. Park just seems plain.

"Yeah, I'm an artist."

"What's your medium?" Her question sounds very precise in her monotone voice.

"Acrylic."

"Ever try oil painting?

"Once…didn't really like it."

"Planning to go to college for art?"

"I wasn't planning on going to college, I just want my art to be shown in museums. I don't feel I need to go to college for that." I feel like I'm in a job interview.

"I see." Ms. Park's eyebrows frown as she's in deep thought. I figure she'll go into a lecture about how important college is. "What do you like to paint?

I'm caught off guard by how she glossed over the fact that I don't plan on going to college. It honestly makes me appreciate her. "I like to paint." I take a slight pause to think about the best way to phrase it. "Beautiful things."

"Okay, paint away." She returns behind the pile of papers she has, and I return to the spot next to Sasha.

"I think that was the longest conversation I've ever seen Ms. Park have."

I don't know how to feel about Ms. Park. At my old school, my art teacher was the only person I could talk to. But what about Ms. Park? What will our relationship be like?

I sit and stare at a large blank canvas while all the other students are busy scribbling away on their projects. "Now what should I paint?"

I like to paint beautiful things. A sunset whose golden orb dips gently below the horizon, casting a warm farewell. The clouds around it shades of pink, orange, and lilac, creating a breathtaking mosaic of colors. A blooming flower whose petals explode out like fireworks. The starry night, a couple holding hands, a kid laughing while chasing bubbles. I paint the beautiful sights in nature.

I know what I want to paint. I would paint the most beautiful thing I've seen since coming here. I open my sketchbook.

Chapter 5

I set up a large canvas in my room and begin to copy the sketch from my book to the blank space. I spent the entire art club hour sketching and planning it out. When I get inspired, nothing can stop me except maybe...

RING RING...RING RING.

I sigh and place my pencil down. "Hi, Mom."

"Sweetie, how are you? How was your first day?"

I rub my temple in annoyance as I make my way to my bed. I was so excited to paint. "It was good."

"Did you make any friends?"

"I actually did." As I think of Chloe and Sasha, a smile finds its way to my lips.

"Wow! I'm so happy to hear about that! I hope the Owens's are treating you well!"

"They are. They're treating me well." I want to say *better than you and Father.* But I don't want to upset her.

"They're not working you too hard?"

"Not since the first day. Not a lot of housework to do at the moment."

"That's good! Oh, your dad just walked in, do you want to talk to him?"

"I would prefer not to talk to my father at the moment."

"Are you sure?"

"Oh, Mom, I gotta go, they're calling me for dinner, talk to you later!" I quickly hang up the phone and sigh, finally turning to my left. "Didn't your parents ever tell you it's not okay to eavesdrop?"

"They may have mentioned it." Zach slides next to me on my bed. "Have daddy issues?"

I roll my eyes. "I would really prefer not to talk about it."

"That's okay. I'm here to listen if you need it." He places his hand over mine. I pull away in disgust.

"I met Maddy. She's beautiful."

"Maddy and I aren't serious or anything."

"Does she know that?"

He has a slick smile. "Don't worry about her. If I talk to her, she won't hurt you."

I mumble under my breath, "I'm worried *for* her, not about her."

Zack throws his wavy hair back and looks at me, waiting for my response.

"I don't remember inviting you into my room."

"Yeah, I know. I was just worried about you."

"Why?" I try to be very direct and serious with him, so he can understand my feelings.

"You're...special..." He runs his fingers through his soft locks while checking to see if I have any response.

"Ick...gross." His face drops at my response.

I feel feet stomping towards us and a hand grabbing me and pulling me to his chest.

"Can't you tell you're making her uncomfortable?" Charlie holds me close, so close I can hear his heart beating. *Uh oh.* I hope Chloe doesn't resent me too much.

Zach lets out a condescending laugh. "Heh, so because you sat with her at lunch you think she's yours?"

I push Charlie away. "I'm not his and I'm certainly not yours."

Zach laughs some more. "Right, I forgot, you're in love with Sam, right?" Zach walks towards the door and shouts for Sam, "Hey, Sam, your lover is looking for you!"

My face becomes beet red at this and my body starts shaking. I run up and push him. "What is the matter with you?"

"What, I'm just trying to be helpful to the happy couple."

"You're acting like a toddler who didn't get their toy!"

Zach is taken aback and tries to think of something to say. "Please, you can like whoever you want." He leans down and puts his face close to mine. "I wouldn't care."

"Is that a promise?"

I become more heated at his condescending attitude. Charlie must pick up on it, too, since he tries to dissolve the situation. "Zach, just drop it, okay? Or are you too dumb to see how upset she is?"

Zach storms over to Charlie. I scream as he grabs his black T-shirt. "What did you say to me?"

Charlie doesn't back down "I called you dumb. Are you too dumb to even understand that word?"

Zach pushes him, "You're just upset since she doesn't like you back. Who's really being a toddler?" Zach pulls back his arm, ready to hit Charlie.

"What are you two doing?" Sam finally arrives and runs between the two. "You're both acting like children!"

"Oh, here to protect your girlfriend." Zach pushes Sam out of the way but Sam pushes back.

"She's not my girlfriend."

Zach pushes Sam even harder, knocking him to the ground. Charlie pushes Zach from behind. "You always do this! You can't stand any girl liking anyone other than you!"

The boys start arguing with one another. Zach and Charlie push each other around while Sam yells at both of them. I have to stop this.

I take a deep breath. "You said you wouldn't care about who I like, right?" I shout over their fighting, hoping to draw their attention. They stop, all eyes on me. "You said I could like anyone, right? Well, I have news for you. I. Like. Girls." Silence. The boys don't respond, but I see their bodies slowly calm down. I can't stop. I'm too angry and the words are coming up like vomit. "I'm a lesbian. I've never felt attracted to boys, I don't think I will ever feel attracted to boys... I like girls. Same as you. I dream about dating girls, kissing girls, and even having sex with girls! So you can stop this petty arguing and get over it since I am not dating *any* of you!"

I stand there trying to catch my breath, my body still trembling. Zach takes a deep breath and simply walks out. "You're too ugly for me anyway." He makes a point of hitting me on the way out, but I won't let him have the last word.

"Hey, Zach." He stops at the door but doesn't turn to face me. "Like I said, Maddy is really beautiful."

He snorts and walks out of the room, shaking his head as he descends the stairs.

I look back to Sam and Charlie, the boys who swore to stay with me. Charlie is silent, deep in his thoughts. After a while he simply walks out without saying anything. Sam gets up next.

"Don't worry about him, he'll get over it. I think he was just surprised, and I don't think he even liked you. I think he was just excited a pretty girl was staying with us." I'm nervous, but Sam flashes me his comforting smile, and I feel the whole world collapse on me. Or that might be because I collapsed. Knowing that he still supports me, tears fill up my eyes. He sits down next to me. "I told you, I'm your friend. I'll be there if you need me.'

And with those words, I let the tears fall from my eyes, gently flow down my cheeks, and crash on Sam's arms, which are embracing me.

Chapter 6

As I wash dishes, I try to avoid looking at my face through the reflection on the faucet. My eyes are still puffy from last night's crying sesh. I felt bad for getting Sam's shirt all wet but, that was the first time anybody had comforted me. The first time someone offered an arm to cry on, the first time I felt safe crying.

Zach and Charlie ignored me all last night and during breakfast. Charlie wouldn't even look at me. I know I shouldn't feel disappointed. Any time I ever confess to someone, someone who I think will really understand, they vanish. I should be used to it by now, but I was really hoping Charlie would be different.

I look into the reflection, ready to see my face, but it's Charlie's face I see. I swing around to face his darting eyes.

"Charlie?" I try not to get my hopes up, try not to want for more. I know what he's going to say, I've prepared myself for it.

"Girls shouldn't like girls, it's wrong. You're wrong. Don't ever show your face in front of me ever again. Don't act like you know me. We. are. Not. Friends."

"I'm sorry." Charlie's usually rough voice sounds soft. "I'm sorry for running away last night. I just had a lot going through my mind."

My eyes widen. The excitement races through me, the hope I repressed starts to resurface.

"I really like you, we all do…and I think my crush on you was mostly due to infatuation, and then hearing that, it snapped me out of it."

I stand there quietly, taking in everything he's saying. Preparing myself for the worst, but praying for the best.

"Thinking about it…I don't have a crush on you or anything. Well, not anymore."

Because you think I'm gross?

"Because I think I see you as more of a friend. I was being honest when I said I'd be there for you. I want to be your friend. Will you be mine?" Charlie's hand reaches out towards me.

I try to appear cool as I grab his hand, but my vision becomes blurry, the tears dripping on my hand.

"I'm sorry! I didn't mean to make you cry again!" I can hear the panic in Charlie's voice.

I laugh as I wipe away my tears. "You didn't make me cry I just…no one has ever been this kind…to…me…" It becomes harder to talk as the tears flow. "U-usually…pe-people…just say that I'm…I'm gross…and…" I can barely manage words between each cry. Snot runs down my nose and my whole face feels moist. "I…I…"

Charlie pulls me into an embrace. I sob loudly into his arms. I feel his hand brushing against the top of my head as he whispers to me, "It's okay…it's okay. We're not going to hurt you…" I breathe deeply into his chest. It feels warm, but a force pulls us apart. Sam puts himself in between us.

"Did you make Michelle cry again? I swear if you made her cry…"

"Sam." I place my hand on his shoulder. "He didn't make me cry." I wipe my tears away. "And please don't hurt my friend. He's very precious." I smile at Charlie and he smiles back.

Sam relaxes. "I'm glad." He smiles. "Let's get you cleaned up for school." He pulls me along and I playfully push him off.

"I can take care of myself…"

"I don't know, I could brush your hair for you, brush your wittle teeth?" Charlie puts on a baby voice as he squishes my face together.

"You guys!" As we walk up the stairs, Zach comes down. He gives us a cold stare, no light in his eyes.

His normally flirtatious voice drops. "Whatever you do, hurry up. We're leaving in five."

Zach is clearly not over it. He rushes by me and takes the passenger seat when we leave. It was only yesterday he was fighting for the back, and now look at him. As we arrive at school, he pops out of the car without saying a word and immediately goes to his friends. They're pointing over to us and laughing. I have a bad feeling in my stomach.

Charlie kicks the door open. "Guess normal Zach is back."

"He's usually like this?"

"He's usually like this with Charlie and I."

"But he's always flirty with the girls." Charlie looks at Zach talking to two girls and rolls his eyes.

I look over, too. My heart starts racing again. *My goddess.* Maddy stands there and quietly watches Zach flirt around with another girl right in front of her. I can tell she's holding back her anger as she looks away. It's then that our eyes lock. Her eyes narrow as she glares at me, scoffs, and looks away. But my heart doesn't calm, it beats for those blue eyes. Even if it was a glare, her eyes sent shivers down my spine.

Sam and Charlie walk in with me. We all notice the eyes and whispers but, unlike yesterday, when I turn towards them, they look away. *Ah, a familiar sight.*

"Michelle!" Ahead I see a comforting sight. My two *friends* Chloe and Sasha. It feels nice to assign them the word *friends*.

"Girlie. We've been looking for you!" Chloe goes into an explosive mood, bursting at the seams to tell me the latest gossip, but as soon as she notices Charlie, she backs down and calms. She has to clear her throat before talking again. "Umm, yeah, we were looking for you." She says this in a nonchalant way, but I can tell she wanted to scream it at the top of her lungs.

Sasha rolls her eyes and pushes her out of the way. "Girl, so, don't freak out, but it got out."

"It?"

Chloe leans in to whisper, "You know, that you're a *lesbian*."

"But I promise we didn't say anything!"

"Yeah, I know you guys didn't say anything." I look at Sam and Charlie who are staring down at the people around us. "I told the boys last night. It was probably Zach who spread it."

Shock creeps its way over their faces. But the shock turns to anger, and then to worry.

"Don't worry." Charlie puts his arm out in front of me like a bodyguard. "If anyone tries to mess with you, we'll beat them up. Right, Sam?"

"As much as I don't usually like violence, the fact that Zach told everyone pisses me off."

"Yeah totally, beat them up!" Chloe puts her arm up and looks to see Charlie's reaction. He simply nods and Chloe's face lights up.

I decide then and there that I will do whatever it takes to get those two together.

"Guys relax, it's fine. People would have found out eventually, it's not like I want to keep it a secret or anything. But…I guess I would have liked people to find out on my terms."

"If that's how you feel we'll respect that, but if you need any one dead…call Charlie." Sam says as he slaps Charlie's back.

"Hey!"

"But I'll also beat some people up for you." Sam smiled at and I smile back.

"Thanks, you guys are the best."

Although I'm used to this, the sight of judging eyes and disapproving whispers, I'm not alone this time. I actually have people there for me, people who will support and fight for me. This time, I won't be afraid.

"I can't believe stupid Zach would just tell everyone like that."

"I can't believe you had a crush on him."

"Girl, I swear if you mention that one more time."

"Honestly, I'm not surprised. Zach's always done shit like this, especially when things don't go his way."

I want to question Charlie more, I want to know the history of the three boys, but the bell rings and now is not the time. I hope one day I can break down their walls.

"Will you be okay getting to your next class?" Sam asks, looking around at the people whispering.

Chloe pops up, saying, "Don't worry, we have most of our classes together so I'll be her classroom protector!"

"Okay, then we'll leave her to you." Charlie gives a thankful smile to Chloe. I think her heart might stop.

"I guess Chloe will take care of Michelle during classes, I'll walk her to lunch, and we can all protect her together during lunch." Sasha said calmly.

The four nod and put their hands in, saying, "Break!"

"Am I included in this or…?" I ask.

"Your job is to be you, and our job is to watch out for you." Sam smiles and tussles my hair.

He walks off as I try to shout at him, "I don't need you to worry about me!"

"Come on, girlie, let's go." Chloe grabs my hand and leads me through the halls.

The whispering gets worse as we go through, and I start to hear Chloe's name whispered. Once I realize what's happening, I stop and pull my hand from Chloe's.

"What's wrong?"

"If people see you holding my hand, they're going to think…"

Chloe grabs my hand back. "Who cares what they think? I'm just looking out for my friend." She once again leads me through the halls.

I didn't know people like this could exist. I never thought anything like this could happen to me. *Chloe, I swear to you I will get you and Charlie together.*

Chapter 7

Chloe really does act as my protector in class. As soon as we sit down people start whispering so she stands up and says, "If anyone has any problems, they can say them out loud!"

"Ms. McGhee, please sit down."

Even though the teacher scolds her, the whispering does stop. It makes class easier for me.

Throughout the morning, the four act as my bodyguards, forming a barrier around me and keeping the crowd away. We're finally able to make it to lunch in one piece.

As we find a table to sit down at, I sit myself down and wave over Charlie. "Charlie! Come sit next to me!" I motion to the spot between Chloe and I. Chloe looks at me, red-faced.

"What are you doing?" she whispers in a hush.

"Repaying the favor from this morning." I give her a wink as Charlie sits between us.

"So, how was the morning?" Charlie begins stuffing his face immediately and I notice Chloe quiet down, but I see a small grin on her face.

"It was good. Thanks to Chloe, no one bothered me!"

Charlie finally turns to face Chloe. "Really? That's awesome! Good job." He holds up his hand for a high five, and I swear I see Chloe's head explode.

"Yeah, I noticed fewer people talking about you, does that have anything to do with you two?" Sasha motions her fry back and forth between Sam and Charlie.

"I may have threatened to beat someone up for talking about you…"

"I may have punched the wall next to someone who was talking about you." The nonchalant way Charlie says that makes me laugh.

"Okay, then." Sam gets serious, pulling us in like a coach going over game tactics. "What's the plan for the afternoon?"

"You *asshole*!" Everyone's attention is pulled to the front of the lunchroom. And when I say everyone, I mean the eyes of everyone in that room go to the front.

At the front of the cafeteria, my goddess is standing up looking at Zach, who is rolling his eyes. I can barely make out him saying, "Jesus, it's not that big of a deal."

My goddess slaps him across the face and storms off, her heels clacking underneath her. Most of the lunchroom is laughing, some are cheering. But all eyes are on Maddy. She holds her head high and goes out with class. At least that's how it looks. It's only for a split second, but I see it, her bottom lip quiver. Just for a moment, but it's there.

Without looking away from her, my body stands and starts walking towards her. I hear Charlie's voice saying, "Where are you going?" but I am too focused on Maddy to look back at him. I follow her as her pace quickens and she disappears into the bathroom.

I approach slowly and hear sniffles coming from the bathroom. My heart hurts for her, and that pain turns towards anger at Zach. How dare he make my goddess cry? I take a deep breath to calm down and fish for my tissues before walking in.

The sight that appears is Maddy looking into the mirror, trying to wipe off her running mascara stains. I approach her slowly. I don't want to scare her, but her head snaps back as she notices me in the mirror.

"What do you want?"

I reach out my hand and present the tissues. "For you."

She scoffs and looks away from me. "No, thanks, I don't need help from a dyke."

I go silent. My eyebrows rise. "Dyke? Haven't heard that one in a while." I turn to leave—there's no helping those who don't want to be fixed.

"Wait." But if there's any chance of wanting to be fixed, I'll take it. "Sorry, I didn't mean that, I was just taking my anger out on you. I'm sorry."

"It's fine, I've heard worse." I once again extend the tissues to her and this time she takes them.

"I guess I should also apologize for what I said yesterday. I clearly had nothing to worry about." She blows her nose into the tissues and the crying begins to stop.

"No, I get it. If someone cheated on me that much, I would probably try picking a fight with every girl I knew."

She looks offended. "Are you trying to make fun of me?"

"No, I'm being honest." I make sure to look directly in her eyes. "Zach's a bad person. Why do you let him make you cry like this?"

Her eyes widen as she turns away in embarrassment. "Why do you care?"

"Because you're too good for him." Maddy freezes. I need to ride this momentum while I have it. "If he hurts you so much, why don't you break up with him?" My eyes plead with Maddy, begging her to open up to me.

"He's mean sometimes…but then he's the sweetest guy you'll ever meet. He'll take me to places he's never taken anyone else, tell me things that only I know, and he always ends up coming back to me. No matter which girl he is with, he always chooses me in the end. He just… He makes me feel like I'm the most special girl in the world."

My mouth hangs open in disbelief. "Are you kidding me? That's literally a textbook example of manipulated abuse! He's abusing you!"

Maddy takes a defensive stance. "He's not abusive! He's never hit me."

I can't stop the words. "Physical abuse isn't the only thing that exists out there. He's toying with your emotions! He's horrible to you, but then the next day makes it up by being sweet. Can't you see he's manipulating you?"

Maddy begins to stumble back. "He's... He's not..."

I should stop but I can't. "There are so many reports about women in abusive relationships who stayed with their abuser because he treated them kindly and promised he would change, but then a couple days later he's back on the same shit again. I bet Zach tells you each time that he'll 'change,' but when has that ever happened?"

Maddy wears a pained expression. I can see the tears forming in her eyes again. *Oh no, I messed up...* She stomps over to me and screams, "You don't know anything!" and storms off, dropping the tissues on the floor.

I sink to the ground. *Shit...I messed up big time.* I put my head in my hands as I think about the words I said to her, how I probably made her feel stupid, how this time I was the one who hurt her. "I'm the one who's not good enough for you..."

"Michelle... What happened?"

I look up to see Chloe and Sasha standing over me. Their breathing tells me they were probably looking for me for a while, their expressions concerned.

"I messed up..."

"Messed up what?" Sasha joins me on the floor, and Chloe follows.

"I messed up with Maddy... I said too much and ended up hurting her." I pull my knees to my chest and lay my head down on them in an attempt to disappear.

"You really like her?"

"Yeah... She's the most beautiful girl I've ever been fortunate enough to lay my eyes on...and I messed everything up." I put my head down again, but roll it towards Sasha. "Sorry, I know she bullied you."

"No, it's okay, but, is Maddy being pretty the only reason you like her? Sasha's question catches me off guard.

"No! of course not! She..." I begin to lose myself in my thoughts. "She has this glow of confidence, she's strong and doesn't back down to people. I admire that..." the room falls silent for a bit. "Right. Sorry, her aggressiveness led to her bullying you."

"At this point I blame Zach more than Maddy" Sasha says to reassure me.

Chloe agrees, "Yeah! Zach is the one to blame, not you!"

"No...I...I said something that made her feel stupid...and now she probably hates me."

"You could apologize." The three of us look up to see Charlie standing at the door.

"Hey, this is the girls' room!" Sasha begins to stand up but Chloe swats at her hand.

"Sorry, I didn't mean to eavesdrop... Well, I guess I should say we..." Charlie nudges his head behind him and Sam pokes his head out from behind Charlie.

"So, you like Maddy?" I nod slowly. "Good, she's too good for Zach, you know she's on honor roll and she's the head cheerleader?"

"Really?"

Sam nods. "Yeah."

"Hey, that reminds me!" Chloe springs up like a lightbulb went off. "We have a game this Friday, maybe you could get her alone after the game and talk to her?"

Sasha stands up, too, offering her hand to me. "We could even help you get alone with her."

I take her hand and she uses her might to pull me up. "Thanks, you guys are the best." I pull Sasha and Chloe in for a hug. "This is platonic by the way…" My friends both laugh. I look towards Sam and Charlie who are waiting at the door. I open up the hug. "Come on, you two."

"Someone said we couldn't come into the girls' bathroom."

"Oh, just get in here." Sasha pulls the boys in for the hug. I notice she makes sure Charlie ends up next to Chloe.

As we break from the hug, Sam speaks up. "So, I guess our next plan is to wait until Friday and then get Michelle alone with Maddy?"

Chloe nods and puts her hand in the middle, followed by Charlie and then Sasha. The group looks towards me.

"You guys are cringe, leave me out of this…" And with that the bell goes off and it's back to classes.

***

When we get home I do some of my housework while the boys go and do whatever it is they do. Zach goes the whole day without saying a single word to me, not that I mind. When I finish, I head up the stairs to continue painting. I finished my sketch so the next step will be to actually get paint onto canvas. Despite everything that happened in the morning and at lunch, the rest of the day was fine. I teased Chloe about how flustered she was in front of Charlie, I did more sketch work with Sasha in art club. I'm beginning to get used to my new life.

"So, Maddy?"

I don't even need to turn to look who it is. Sam and Charlie would have knocked, but Zach just barges in.

"What about her?"

"I saw you run after her."

I don't acknowledge him, I just keep dipping my brush into the paint and creating strokes against my canvas. "As her boyfriend, isn't it your job to run after her... Also I thought you didn't want to talk to me anymore."

"It's not like that, I just didn't know how to react..."

"Is that why you told the whole school?"

I don't hear Zach respond for a while, but I also don't want to give him the satisfaction of looking his way. "Maddy is straight, you know..."

"And...?"

"And what?"

"What's your point in telling me something I already know?"

"So you can stop pursuing her?" I can sense the anger building in Zach's voice.

"Who said I'm pursuing her?"

"Ha, so you following after her was just an act of kindness? You sure you didn't have any ulterior motive?"

I finally stop and place my brush back into my water cup. I take my time placing my paint tray on the ground before walking to Zach, who has a smug expression on.

I look him dead in the eye. "You will never be good enough for that girl." I start pushing on his chest. "Now go, get out of my room!"

As I am shoving him out, he has one last retort. "Do your parents know?"

I don't bother answering him. I slam the door shut and collapse on my bed. I look up at my ceiling fan and think of Maddy. "I promise, Maddy…I will save you."

Just three more days until the game. I just need to wait three more days.

Chapter 8

The student body is decked out in blue and white, the cheerleaders walk proudly in the hall, showing off their uniforms, and the football players goof off in class, using the excuse of, "Saving energy for the game." My old school didn't go this crazy for a Friday football game, although we didn't really care about our football team. The only time we would go crazy would be for the Eagles.

In class Chloe taps on my shoulder. "Are you excited for tonight?"

I raise an eyebrow and decide to tease her a bit. "Are you?"

Her face flushes. "Me? What would I be excited about?"

"I don't know, maybe how we'll all be going together and sitting together... You... Me... Sasha... Sam... Oh, and Charlie said he can't make it."

She slams her hands down on her desk. "What!"

"Ms. McGhee, if you don't understand the problem, just raise your hand like a normal person."

I feel bad watching Chloe apologize; that was enough teasing for the day. "I'm kidding, of course he'll be there, and at the bonfire afterwards, you two could sit next to each other..." I notice Chloe's cheeks getting pinker. "Cuddle up next to the fire..." Getting redder. "Maybe you can rest your head on his shoulder..."

She finally stands up. "No *way*!"

"Once again, Ms. McGhee, you will need to solve these problems by the end of class."

I have to cover my mouth to stop laughing. Chloe slinks down into her chair. "You really are an asshole sometimes."

"Yes, but that's part of my charm."

Chloe snorts. "yeah, I guess I can keep you around a bit longer."

The five of us have gotten a lot closer over the week. Sasha has begun to show me some of her sketch work—she's one of those artists who won't show you her work until it's finished. I got to watch Sam make a small bench. During art club, I snuck out to meet him. He took me into the woodshop room and I just sat there and watched him work. I enjoyed watching how much focus he had on his face, how much persuasion he had in his fingers. The whole time he was focused on his craft, I was reminded of how focused I become when I paint.

"You and I are very similar," I said to him.

Sam looked up at me. "Are you saying I'm a lesbian?"

"Hoho, look who developed a sense of humor."

"Must have learned it from you." He went back to sanding his bench.

"Do you want to do woodwork professionally?"

"I don't know…never really thought about it. Always considered it a hobby."

"Seriously? Then what do you want to do for work?"

"I'll probably go to Ohio State, get a business degree, and start working at my dad's company."

"Paul sells electrical supplies, right?" I ask.

"Yeah, his company basically sells electrical supplies to other companies."

"You're going to waste your talent selling electronics?"

"It's my talent, I can waste it however I like." Sam laughed it off like a joke, but I only found it sad.

"You should sell your work. Start a business. That's what I would do if I were you."

"Sounds nice to be you." I felt there was nothing I could do for Sam at that moment. I could see the passion in his eyes—he couldn't give it up. But there was only so much I could do for him. I didn't want to push him like I did Maddy, but I was hoping slowly, I could break down his walls.

I got to learn more about Charlie as well.

"Hey, can I come see your band practice?" I asked him one afternoon.

Charlie whipped his head around. "Who told you I was in a band?"

"I have my sources."

"Don't come see my practice…it's too embarrassing!" He walked faster, but I caught up.

"You should tell me when you have a live show."

"Oh, you are *not* coming to my live show."

"Please, your fans want to see you."

"Oh, you're my fan now?" Charlie sped up.

"I didn't say me…you're a lot more liked than you think."

Charlie finally stopped; it was so sudden I bumped into his back.

"I'm not well liked…and even if I was, he wouldn't allow it." After his comment he began walking away.

He didn't say who, but I knew it was Zach. "Is he also the reason you don't want people to see you play?" He didn't answer. I caught up to him and gave him a back hug, my hands meeting at his stomach. "When you're ready, please invite me to see your show."

It took a while, but he finally said, "Okay" in such a quiet voice I didn't know if I imagined it or not.

I'm glad I got to know my friends more. Spending time with them also distracted me from the looks I've been getting from Maddy. She and I would make eye contact, and she would deliberately look away. Each time a crack formed in my heart.

I wish I could approach her, I wish I could scream, "I didn't mean it, you're my goddess!" But I can't. It doesn't help that Zach guards her anytime I get near. I just need to make it 'til tonight.

"Because Zach is staying after school for the game, we get the car all to ourselves." Charlie throws back some fries. "Wee shwuld ko ofher."

"Charlie, chew before speaking." Sam turns to address the group. "I think what my dumbass brother was saying is that we should all go together."

I take this opportunity. "Yeah, I'll sit up front with Sam, and Chloe, Sash, and Charlie can sit in the back!" I can tell Chloe wants to scream after hearing this. I hope she appreciates the work I'm putting in for her.

"So, I guess, meet at our car after school?"

"Yeah, there's actually this cool ice cream place in town we can stop by..." As my friend's voices go on, they blur together. I sit there as if I'm watching a play from the audience. A play about four average friends making plans to hang out after school and laughing together. It's a play that I'll watch but never be a part of...

"Michelle... Michelle?" I snap out of my deep thought to see everyone staring at me, Sam calling my name.

"Yeah..."

"We were asking if there was anything you wanted to do…"

"Oh… I…" I'm a part of this play, aren't I? I'm not just watching a friend group have fun together. I'm a part of this group, and I'm having fun with them. "Is there an art store nearby?"

Charlie bursts out laughing "Don't you already have like a million art supplies?"

"Yeah, but I could always use more."

Charlie leans into the group to whisper, "I think she might have a spending problem…"

"I do not!!"

That's right… This isn't even a play, this is just reality. In reality, I have friends who care for me, friends who actually want me around…and most of all, friends who accept me for who I am.

Chapter 9

"Gooo, Big Blue! Goooo, Big Blue!"

"Oh god, I think she's drooling…" I feel Sasha's hand close my mouth, which hangs open. My goddess looks amazing in her cheerleading uniform. She has the most energy out of all of the girls on the field, and the most talent. At one point she does a back handspring into a back tuck and I almost faint.

"I thought I knew beauty until I saw Maddy Vitis in a cheerleading uniform."

"So, are cheerleaders your type?" Charlie nudges me while asking.

"Maddy is my type." I stare blankly without taking my eyes off of her.

"I can't believe you're into her."

"What? You never were?"

Charlie's cheeks flush. "I mean, I feel like every guy had a crush on her at one point!"

"I didn't."

"No one asked you, Sam. But it was like a celebrity crush, no one actually thought they would ever be with her so they moved on."

I look at Charlie and notice a morose Chloe sitting next to him. She probably doesn't appreciate hearing about Charlie's crush on Maddy.

"Well, maybe Maddy just wasn't the one for you, maybe there are other girls who you won't be able to get over."

"Are you saying you'll never get over Maddy?"

"Don't bring my goddess into this. And besides, the only thing I want for Maddy… I want to save her."

"You say that like Zach is some evil monster who has a hold on her…"

"He does!" me, Charlie, Sam and Chloe all shout at the same time.

"I knew it! You still have a crush on him!"

"Girl, turn around because I'm about to whoop your ass." Sasha stands up and tries to push Chloe over, but Chloe put her hands up in defense.

"Wait wait, no I'm sorry!"

"Calm down, you two."

"Okay, Michi!" Chloe sits back down next to Charlie.

"Michi?"

"Your nickname!"

"I don't like it."

"Too bad, it's my nickname for you. You don't get a say." Chloe gives a *you don't get a choice* look.

"I like Michi, too, it's cute," Sam decides to chime in. "Can I call you that, too?"

"I never gave Chloe permission to call me that."

"Hey, Michi, I'm going to get a hot dog. Do you want anything?"

"Charlie, not you, too."

"Hey, Michi." Sasha's head appears next to mine "What's the plan for after the game?"

I guess nothing I can say will stop my new nickname. Michi sounds too childish. But deep down, part of me is excited for my first-ever nickname.

"I think the best action would be to catch her before she heads back into the locker room, like behind the bleachers."

"Okay, do you think maybe we could find a way to get her behind the bleachers?" Sam stares, deep into thought.

Chloe pipes up, "We could take one of her pom-poms or her gym bag?"

"The pom-poms might actually work," Charlie adds in, making Chloe go shy again as he agrees with her plan. "If I remember, at the end of the game they throw their pom-poms up. If we can try to catch one and throw it behind the bleachers, it should work."

"That…is a great idea Charlie," Chloe says in a sweet voice, her finger twirling around in her hair.

"Thanks, I only thought of it because you mentioned the pom-poms." Charlie smiles at Chloe, and my eyebrow raises—*Oh, Is Charlie showing some affection?*

"Okay, that sounds like a good plan. Michi, are you on board?" I cringe at Sam calling me Michi, but it's a good plan.

"Yeah, I trust you guys, thank you for helping me with this."

Sasha hits me on the back. "Stop thanking us, it's what friends do."

"Honestly, I'm just in it to hurt Zach." We all stare at Charlie who is casually leaning back on the bench. "What? He hates losing things that are his. If we take Maddy away, he'll be pissed. I want to see him pissed off." A sinister smile creeps onto Charlie's face. I don't know what happened between Charlie and Zach, but as long as Charlie is helping me with Maddy, that's all I need to know. When Charlie is ready, I'm sure he'll tell me all about it.

The game is boring. Anytime the cheerleaders aren't doing anything, I'm just drawing, but as soon as my goddess appears, my eyes are glued.

"She's drooling again…" Once again Sasha has to close my mouth.

The crowd stands up and Charlie grabs me to stand up, too. "This is it, this is when they'll throw the pom-poms!"

I watch carefully as the last cheer is performed.

"WHO'S GOT THE DYNAMITE? WE KNOW WE GOT THE DYNAMITE! WHO'S GOT THE DYNAMITE? WE GOT THAT TICK TICK TICK BOOM!" The cheerleaders throw their pom-poms up. In the mess, Sam reaches forward and grabs two random pom-poms.

He hurries back over to us and drops the pom-poms under the bleachers. "How do you know they were Maddy's?"

"I don't, but she's the head cheerleader, she'll be responsible for all of the pom-poms anyway."

I can't help but to grab Sam's face. "You are the best!"

He smiles and pushes me off. "Now go, say what you need to say to her."

I nod. I look towards my other friends who all give me a thumbs-up, and run under the bleachers.

My heart is going crazy, beating so hard I get nervous other people can hear me. What if she's still mad? What if this only makes her hate me more? I take deep breaths and close my eyes. I listen to the sounds of footsteps walking off the bleachers, sounds of dirt being kicked around under their sneakers. I hear the sounds of cars driving off in the distance, probably heading to the bonfire, and then I hear what I'm waiting for.

"Hey, Maddy, I can't find my pom-poms."

"Ugh, That's why I told you guys not to throw them too far."

"I know! I'm sorry! I'll look for them now."

"Forget it, you're a freshman so I'll let you off the hook, but next time, expect to run ten laps, okay?"

"Ugh! Okay! Sorry! Thank you!" Footsteps run by. I open my eyes and pick up the pom-poms.

I turn to face Maddy who is already behind me. "Are you looking for these?"

"What are you doing here?" She already has a hostile tone as she rips the pom-poms from me.

"I came to apologize about the other day... I shouldn't have said those things to you... I'm sorry. You're not...stupid or anything " I don't know what I'm saying. I can't even look her in the eyes. I just need to say something. "I messed up. I'm sorry."

I stare directly at the ground. I won't be able to handle it if Maddy is still upset with me. I stay there waiting to hear her footsteps leave me, but instead her sneakers appear in my line of vision. I look up to see her only a few feet away from me. Her makeup is stunning. It's neutral tones, but each of them are shimmering. She even has shine in her blush. I think about how at this moment, she really looked like a goddess.

"It's okay, you weren't wrong anyway." Hearing this, my body collapses. I spent the whole week stressing over this, fearing that my love was over before it began, but hearing those words, a giant weight is lifted from me.

I can't relax yet. I don't want to mess this up again. "Still, it wasn't right speaking up about something I didn't know about...and the last thing I wanted to do was make you more upset."

Maddy sighs and leans her back against the bleachers. "I honestly thought about everything you said...I even looked up emotional abuse and manipulation and you were right..." Maddy laughs to herself. "I'm literally the textbook example of manipulation in abuse."

I walk over and lean back next to her. "But you know it's not *you*, right?"

"Yeah...it's Zach... He sucks." My eyes pop up in disbelief. Is she really admitting it? Have I actually saved Maddy? "But I still love him." The reality crushes me again. I knew it would take a lot more than that to save her. "Thank you for trying to help me, but I want to figure this out on my own. I want to hope that the man I fell in love with is still in there." I shudder as she says "man I fell in love with," but at the same time, I have to respect her decision.

I nod. "Okay, just, stay safe out there... Your makeup is too pretty to be ruined because of a prick like him."

Maddy laughs a genuine laugh. Her laugh is everything I thought it would be. Light and contagious, filling the air with its warmth, infecting me with joy.

"Are you going to be at the bonfire tonight?" I freeze. The way she says it sounds like she's inviting me. I suddenly remember that I'm talking to a goddess and begin to sweat a bit.

"Yeah, I mean...I was planning on it...maybe... ahaha." I do not do the best job at hiding how nervous I am. I can also tell she can tell. I'm ready for embarrassment but she just smiles.

She turns on her heels to walk off. "See you there, new girl."

"Michelle!" I catch her right before she leaves. "My name is Michelle."

"Michelle?"

Hearing her call my name makes me lose my nerve all over again. "Yeah...but my friends call me Michi!" *Crap, why did I blurt that out!*

"Michi? That's so cringe, I don't like it." She officially turns and walks off. I watch and wait. Wait until she is completely out of sight before jumping up and down with joy.

"Yes, yes, *yes*!" My mouth starts to hurt by how wide my smile is. I keep cheering to myself, running through the conversation over and over again. "She also thinks Michi is cringy!" I keep jumping. I need to get out all of the energy I'm feeling. After a short five-minute freak out, I collect myself and head towards the parking lot. My friends are patiently waiting for me at the car. It warms my heart to think they waited all this time. I also take note of Chloe being able to have an actual conversation with Charlie. *I'll make sure to tease her about that later.*

I walk up, trying to seem casual. "Hey, guys."

They stare at me, waiting for something. Finally, Chloe steps forward. "Well? How did it go?"

I wait for a moment, letting the anticipation grow. I revel in my friend's faces as they wait to either celebrate with me or comfort me. I finally let my smile show. "She forgave me!"

"Yay!" Chloe, Sasha, and I all huddle together, jumping and screaming in excitement.

"Oww, my ear drums." Charlie comically holds his ears as if they're bleeding.

Chloe and Sasha calm down, but I want to tell them more. "She also asked if I would be at the bonfire tonight."

"Oh my god!" The jumping and screaming starts again. I hear Charlie groan in the background.

I feel a warm hand pat my back. "I'm glad that was resolved, I know how much this had been bothering you."

I turn to the familiar smile. "Thanks, Sam." I pull him into a hug next. "You're the best."

"Hey, what about us?" Sasha gestures to the rest of the group.

"You guys are the best…just…the second best." As I hear complaints from the crowd, I slide into the passenger seat and wait for Sam to get in and start the car.

"You think you'll be okay at the bonfire? Zach will be there, and he'll probably be hooking up with Maddy in front of you."

"I know, and I'm ready for that. I also trust Maddy to make the right decisions."

The others file into the car and we're off. I don't know what to expect from the bonfire. Will Maddy really be able to talk to Zach about it, and if she does, will he even listen? I want to trust Maddy, and I don't want to stick my nose where it doesn't belong…but I'm worried about her, afraid something bad might happen at the campfire tonight.

Chapter 10

"Let's go Patriots! Let's go to states this year! Whoo!" The crowd of drunken teens all raise their red Solo cups and cheer with the already plastered football star standing on a table. We watch as he chugs…chugs…chugs…and falls off the table.

"They do realize that our team lost, right?" Sasha says, sipping on a soda. She explained that she wasn't a fan of drinking and wanted to make a statement by never drinking.

"They didn't?"

"Michi, were you not paying attention to the game?"

I give a side eye to Sasha. "Did it look like I was paying attention?"

"You're right, I should have known better."

We clang our cups together and sip. I decided to be brave and try the "jungle juice" someone brought…and I regret my decision after that one sip.

"Gross…I'm going to throw this out."

Sasha raises her cup and I walk off. I take this opportunity to survey my surroundings. We're in a clearing in the dense forest, the colossal bonfire crackling in the center, its flames casting an amber glow on the faces of teenagers gathered around it. Sam had volunteered to look after the fire, and he takes his job very seriously. I watch as he stomps around the whole perimeter of the fire, checking to make sure each corner is lit up. As he fans the flames, kids get closer to it, but he shoos them away so as to not mess up the fire in any way.

I'm delighted to see Chloe and Charlie standing a few feet from the fire, both holding drinks and laughing. It feels like just yesterday she could barely look at him, but now she's throwing her head back laughing with him. I think to myself how they make a cute couple, the shy musician with the outgoing girlie girl; it's like something out of those cheesy romance books.

I make my way to a trash can…or I should say trash bag overflowing on the ground with cups, bottles, cans, and god knows what else. In the corner of the clearing, I see the football players and cheerleaders huddled around a keg. Maddy is standing there smiling with Zach's arm around her shoulder. I hope she was able to talk to him and he apologized, or I hope that he'll at least try to treat her better now, but from the eyes he's giving to a girl across the circle, I know he won't. What breaks my heart more is watching that girl give a look to Zach, and walking off into the woods. I can barely see Zach mouth, "I'm going to go to the bathroom for a bit," before following after her. I begin to shake. *That prick is going to make my goddess cry again.* I carefully watch Maddy, looking to see if I can see her bottom lip quiver, but instead I see something worse. I see her start to move into the woods after them.

No no no no no no. I won't let Zach do this again…not to Maddy, not after seeing how sure she was about how he would change after she talked to him. I feel my pace quicken and suddenly, without even realizing it, I had caught up to Maddy. My hand wraps around her wrist. She stops walking, but she doesn't look at me. She's waiting for me to do something…to say something…

There are a million things I want to say, but all that comes out is, "Don't." Don't go and cause yourself more pain… You don't need to see what's happening in those woods, it would only do more damage.

Maddy raises her head in thought. I wish I could see what face she's making. I wish I could see if she's hurting or not, if she's mad at me for following her again, but all I get is a release of air and her hand flipping and grabbing my wrist.

"Come with me." She turns away from the direction Zach had headed to and leads me down another path. I don't resist at all, the path is clear and lit up by the moon above. She walks as if she walked this path a million times over. At the end of the path is a river, a river flowing past large boulders surrounding it. Maddy stands there showing it to me, her hand still wrapped around my wrist.

"This is where Zach would take us on our dates. He told me it was his secret place that only I knew, and it made me feel special...until I heard one of the other cheerleaders talking about this spot...and how Zach took her here." I feel her hand tighten on my wrist. As she's talking, I stand and listen. She's not talking to get advice, she's talking to be heard, and I will gladly hear anything she has to say. "Zach was an idiot though. He didn't realize that just a few feet in that direction, you get an even better view."

Still holding my wrist, she leads me across the river and through the trees. This time the path is not as clear, and we are pushing away several branches to get out, but when we finally make it out, before me lays a wide open field, sprawled endlessly, a sea of swaying grasses beneath the open sky. Maddy finally lets go of my wrist and sprints into vast space.

I can only stand there, too in awe of the beauty to do anything. The only thing that snaps me out of my trance is Maddy's playful voice. "Come on!" *You don't need to ask me twice.*

I sprint off after her, feeling the wind in my hair, a sense of freedom washing over me. The field seems endless, like we could keep running forever and ever.

I eventually catch up with Maddy who collapses on her back, looking up to the sky. I instinctively follow her lead. The grass feels soft under my touch, like lying on a blanket of wool, each grass blade gently pressing up against me.

I already think the sight is amazing, but as I look up to the sky, I am stunned all over again. The night sky looms above the open field like an expansive canvas splattered with innumerable stars. A tapestry of darkness embellished by celestial bodies, it stretches endlessly, each star a tiny, twinkling luminary amidst the vast expanse. The moon, a radiant pearl, casts its silver glow, lighting up the entire space.

"This is amazing," I say through heavy breathing. I'm not used to running. "I never knew we had this many stars in our sky!"

"Really? Have you never seen an open sky before?"

"Not living in Philly my whole life. With all the lights of the city, we're lucky to see one or two stars in the sky."

"So, you're a city girl?" I notice something strange in Maddy's tone. She asks the question as if only pretending to care, but her mind is completely elsewhere.

I turn my head to look at her. She's breathing heavily, but not from the running, and she curls her lips in. I recognize this look; it's something I have done all my life.

"You don't have to keep it in… If you need to cry, then cry." I use a soft tone when speaking to her. I can see how fragile she is at the moment and I don't want to rush her.

I finally hear her voice start to quiver. "I thought you said you didn't want me to ruin my makeup by crying over him."

I stare at her as she struggles to keep her tears down. *I messed up again.* "If…if this will be the last time, then you should cry all you want. Keeping it in won't help you." She finally turns her head towards me. "There's no one around, you can cry as loud as you want."

I watch as tears well up, her features soften, and the dam of emotions breaks, flowing down her cheeks. It starts as a small silent cry, but as more tears stream down her face, the sobs get louder. I nudge myself closer to her and pull her head into my shoulder, letting her cry even louder. She's letting everything out, four years of emotional abuse, of pretending everything was okay, of playing the villain in everyone's story—she lets it all out in one night.

I don't know how long she cries for. As she sobs into my shoulder I watch the sky, the constellations moving with the time going by, the night accompanied by the sound of crickets and fall leaves blowing in the wind. Soon the crying stops, and Maddy sits up, rubbing her eyes.

I sit up with her. "Do you feel better?"

Maddy blows her nose on the sleeve of her brown leather jacket. "Yeah…but I think my makeup is all ruined now." She looks towards me, presenting her damp face with running makeup.

My heart skips a beat. "You look beautiful right now."

She scoffs, "Yeah right."

I put my hand over hers to grab her focus.

"No really…" I place my hand on her cheek, examining her like a work of art. "You look beautiful."

I'm not someone who lies to make people feel better, I tell them how I feel, even when they don't want to hear it…usually when they don't want to hear it…and I can't lie to Maddy. Her shimmering eye shadow has streamed down, covering her whole face in sparkles, made to shine even more in the pale moonlight. Her running mascara looks like tear drops made of deep obsidian crystals.

I whip my phone out and use the reflection to show her her face. "See, you have this sort of angelic look."

She stares at her reflection and tries to wipe the glitter off her face. "I don't know what you're seeing, I look like a mess."

"Well, beauty is in the eye of the beholder."

"You look pretty, too…here." She grabs my phone and tries to hold it to my face but I push it away.

"No! I don't wanna see my face!"

"Why? You look nice in the moonlight!"

"No!" We fight as she tries to show the phone to my face and I try to keep it away. As we tussle, we eventually fall on our backs again, laughing as we feel the soft grass.

"Thank you for letting me cry tonight."

"It's good to cry; if you keep it in for too long, you'll end up exploding later…literally you'll burst into flames." I add the last part with a hint of sarcasm.

Maddy gets to laugh after a night of crying, and I feel a sense of triumph watching her lie in the grass with a smile on her face. I'm glad I was able to get her mind off of that prick for a while. We lie there in silence for a while, watching the sky and feeling the breeze. I would be okay staying like this forever.

Maddy rolls over to face me. I roll over to face her, not realizing how close our faces are. I start to get nervous again, worried she will hear my heartbeat from this close.

She stares at me for a while. The more her eyes peer into mine, the quicker my heartbeat gets. If this goes on for any longer I might have a heart attack.

"We should go back." Her voice sounds like the whisper you hear in the morning, when the world is still asleep, and the slightest sound can awaken everyone.

I can't say any words to her, I just nod and follow her. Just like how we got here, she leads me through the woods, only this time she holds my hand instead of my wrist.

By the time we get back, most people had left. The first thing I see is Sam carefully putting out the fire. I chuckle at the thought of how dedicated Sam was to this fire. I'll ask him later if he was ever a Boy Scout.

Charlie, Chloe, and Sasha are standing near the fire talking, probably waiting for me, but they don't seem too concerned. Who I don't see anywhere is Zach.

I look to Maddy who is scanning the clearing. "Do you have a ride?"

"I drove myself...actually I drove a lot of people here, but I don't see them anywhere. I guess I'll drive home on my own."

"Good, make them walk home." I say with a smile.

"Ha, if only, those bitches probably left without me."

"Then they missed out."

Maddy smiles, an image that I burn into my brain. She finally lets go and walks off. "See you, Michelle."

My eyes widen and my head pops up in surprise. Just when I thought she couldn't make my heart skip any more, she calls out my name as she leaves. *This was the best day of my life...*

I stand frozen, watching her disappear to the patch of land all the cars are parked on. Only about four cars remain, ours included, but as people pull out, only our car remains.

"Miiiiichhi!" I feel a small body jump on me.

"Chloe, I have at least ten more years until I start getting back pain, please don't make me start early."

She puts her arm around me and pulls me close. "I saw you with Maddy, is that who you disappeared with?"

I whisper back to her, "Maybe... I saw you talking with Charlie, are you making any progress?"

She pulls away from me, flustered. "That's...we're talking about you right now!"

"Okay okay, I'll tell you about it later, okay?"

"Okay!" Chloe runs back to Sasha to probably tell her the news.

I take a moment to look up; the stars are harder to see here since there are so many trees around, only a sliver of sky peeking out amongst the tall treetops. The view is nothing compared to what Maddy showed me. *Maddy.* I can't get her out of my head. I look back to the group. "Guys, come on, I wanna get home!"

"What, you don't like hanging with us?"

"Not that, but I just really need to paint right now!"

Sasha chuckles. "I get that feeling. Come on, guys, let's get this crazy girl home."

Being surrounded by trees is a new experience, having friends in a new experience, having a crush on someone who doesn't find me gross is a new experience; there are so many things I've gotten to experience for the first time in my eighteen years of living, and it's only been a week! As I move on with the school year, I ponder what more I will get to experience.

Chapter 11

"So, did you guys kiss?"

Chloe's red face is something I enjoy seeing every morning in class. "No! We just talked and stuff..."

"Yeah, but he seemed really into the conversation." I nudge her and in a sing-song voice say, "He was laughing with you, and staring at you, and..."

"Okay stop! I'm too embarrassed!"

"We should totally get him to invite us to one of his practices! Don't you wanna see him jam out? Looking all cool on his guitar?"

Chloe gives a small smile as she wiggles in her chair. "I don't know, maybe..."

"Then ask him to invite us!"

"No! You ask him! You're the one living with him!"

"I've asked him already and he said no."

"Then why would he say yes to me?"

"Umm, because he likes you...duh?"

"He!" Chloe is close to shouting during class again but catches herself. "He doesn't like me..."

I can only give a deadpan stare to Chloe. Is she messing with me or does she really not notice?

"Well, what about you and Maddy? Do you think she likes you?"

I can't help but laugh to myself at the question. It's obvious she won't have romantic feelings for me…but I get what Chloe's asking.

"She doesn't seem to hate me."

"That's a start!"

"Chloe…" I sigh as I try to find the best way to say this. "I'm not doing this in the hopes that Maddy will one day feel the same way about me and we'll start a relationship."

"You don't know that—"

"But I do know that." I've experienced it countless times before. "I just want to make sure she doesn't get hurt anymore, that's all."

Chloe puts her hand on my arm to comfort me. "You're a very good person."

In the same comforting tone, I respond, "I pushed Charlie down the stairs this morning, you should comfort him."

Chloe follows the tone. "Why are you like this?"

"It gives me joy… Also I didn't actually push Charlie down the stairs, but you should still check on him."

I enjoy watching Charlie and Chloe's relationship grow. They are both dear friends of mine who I care about, and seeing them happy together is the best way I can repay them for what they've done for me. I wish there were ways I could help Sasha and Sam. I don't see Sasha much since I only see her during class, lunch, and art club, so there's not a lot I can do for her at the moment, but she also seems like a confident girl. She's one of the only people of color at our school so she already stands out, but just to prove a point she dyes her hair, wears bright makeup and mismatched outfits.

When I asked her why she simply said, "If I'm gunna stand out anyway, I would rather do it on my own terms."

She doesn't seem like someone who needs anyone to help her or to lend a shoulder to cry on; most of the time we just sit next to each other and paint in silence.

Sam, on the other hand, is a bit more complicated. We've gotten much closer, especially since we live together, but I feel he's not letting me in completely yet. Same with Charlie—there's something there that the boys just aren't ready to share with me yet, but I'm fine waiting. We have a whole year together.

• •

"Alright, students, I have an announcement to make."

Sasha and I peek our heads over our easels to see a once-in-a-blue-moon event, Ms. Park actually addressing the art club. The five of us exchange looks of confusion and a bit of terror. It's been a few weeks since school has started and other than the first day, Ms. Park has only ever greeted me, but now here she is at the front of the classroom, addressing five shy art kids who come to club since it's one of the only places they can create safely.

"There's a contemporary art museum in Dayton that's offering some spots in their next exhibit to high school students."

I embarrass myself by gasping out loud, but my dream of having a work of mine shown in a museum is within reach! Even if it's some small museum in Dayton, Ohio, that's a start.

Ms. Park clears her throat. "I know some of you may seem excited about this"—she looks directly at me—"but know that this is open to all Ohio high schools, and they only have a few spots… So think about if you really want to submit something, and if you do, make sure it's your best work."

The group stares blankly at Ms. Park. I can tell she's not used to addressing students. She's choppy with her wording and stands up at the front of the classroom like a statue. We all just wait for her to finish her painfully awkward speech.

"The deadline is next month on the fifteenth… You have a little over a month to think of something you want to submit. And it doesn't need to be new. If you have an old project you are very confident about, you can submit that…"

The class is silent.

"Anyway, if you have something you would like to submit, please see me after club ends. Thank you."

And with that, she's back to hiding behind her desk. The room holds its breath for a moment, taking in the event that just unfolded, but eventually we all just go back to our own projects.

"Are you going to submit anything?" Sasha asks.

"Nah, it's not like it's been my dream to have one of my pieces shown in a museum, and it's not like I gasped after the announcement, I'm not interested at all…" Sasha narrows her eyes and gives me a "seriously?" look.

"I have a few things in mind I want to submit. There's actually something I've been working on since I first got here, I should be finished with it before the deadline."

"Oh yeah? The one you've been spending hours in your room working on?"

"How do you know about that?"

"Sam and Charlie."

"Right… What about you?"

Sasha hesitates for a bit, resting her paintbrush on her mouth as she thinks. "Probably not. I've never been interested in showing my art in a museum or anything. I want to be a commission artist."

"The kind that paints whatever people ask them to?"

"Yeah. When I was younger I always liked to draw, and my family would ask me to draw all sorts of things for them. I think they were just asking for fun, let a little girl run her own make-believe art shop." I turn all of my focus to Sasha—it's the first time I've heard her talk about her past. "As I drew more I got better, and soon, I was actually able to draw what people asked me to. Suddenly it went from a game to them to actually something to be proud of. I started getting requests from my family's friends and coworkers and well…"

"You found your passion?"

"I found a way I could make money."

"Oh yes, of course."

We share a nice laugh. "I wanted to keep practicing art so I could really create what people wanted, and if it's not perfect I'll just restart."

"That's a lot of money for one mistake."

"Says the girl who spent three hundred dollars on paints she probably already owns!"

"I may have an issue…but anyway, do you have a website or something?"

"Not yet, currently I get commissions from referrals, and I'm saving that money to go to art school, and then I'll have my own website."

"Wow, you really have things figured out…"

"Not always, though… It took me a while to get here."

I want to hear more about Sasha's past, she rarely ever talks about it. I hear all about Chloe's escapades as a child, but never Sasha's. I was going to ask her about why it took her a while to get to where she is and how she did it, but her headphones are in now, which means our conversation is over. Even if it was a little, I'm glad I was able to see into Sasha's life.

As the clock strikes 4:30, was time to move on and meet the boys. Sasha gets her belongings collected and is ready to rush out. "Ready?"

"No, I'm going to talk to Ms. Park about the museum, I'll catch you tomorrow." She motions to a chair, saying she could wait, but I wave her off, leaving just me and Ms. Park.

"Hi…Ms. Park." I speak rather quietly since I'm not used to speaking to her and I don't know how she'll reply.

"Yes, the one who gasped. Are you going to submit an old piece or think of something new?" Ms. Park is very direct and gets straight to the point. That's one of the things I like about her—she doesn't bullshit things, and she lets us do whatever we want in class.

"I actually have something I've been working on for a while that I want to submit."

Without even looking up at me Ms. Park responds, "Good. Just let me know when it's finished and we can work on the submission papers." And with that she waves me off and gets back to work.

I shrug and head out into the hallway, the excitement starting to build in me, and I skip through the halls with glee, a dumb smile plastered across my face. I see Sam leaving the woodshop room, and I quickly run over and link up with his arm. "Sam, Sam! Guess what?"

I explain everything on the way to the parking lot. "Really? That's awesome! You've been working really hard on that painting in your room! Also, does this mean I can finally see the painting?"

"Hmm, I guess, but not until it's hanging in the museum, okay?"

"Alright, deal." He puts out his pinky and I wrap mine around it, making the deal complete.

As we enter the parking lot, I see Charlie already waiting by the car, his guitar case leaning up against the door.

I run straight to Charlie with the exciting news.

"That's awesome! You'll have to be picked—if not then the whole thing was rigged from the start."

"Oh, my piece will be picked, I'm feeling even more motivated now. I shall start painting 'til dawn!"

"Yeah, please don't do that to yourself." Sam pats my head, letting me know to take it easy. His kindness is something I will never take advantage of.

"Hey, losers." Zach waltzes over and pushes us out of the way to get to the passenger seat door.

"You can say excuse me, you know?" Zach doesn't respond to me, he just swings open the door and throws his stuff in. I'm ready to get in the car when I hear heels tapping towards us. My heart flutters at the sound. "Maddy!"

When Zach notices Maddy, he walks towards her with a cocky smile. "Hey, babe, here to see me off?" But she pushes past him, barely giving him a glance, and walks right to me.

"Hey, Michelle."

Hello, my goddess. "Hi."

Since the bonfire, Maddy and I have exchanged greetings in the hallways. We haven't had any conversations or anything, but if we pass each other in the hall we will say hi. This development is new; this is the first time she's sought me out.

"Wanna go into town with me? And not our boring town. Saint Paris is like an hour-long drive from here. They've got some cute stores and nice restaurants we can go to."

I stand there like a deer caught in headlights, wondering if I'm in a dream or some alternate dimension. Charlie nudges me forward and I am broken from my trance.

"Uh… Yeah, sure. Let's…"

"Cool, let's go." She pivots and heads towards her car, right past a stunned, wide-mouthed Zach. I quickly follow after her since I don't want to get Zach's wrath. As we get closer to her small silver Audi, I hear Zach yell, "Really, Maddy?" But she completely ignores him and gets into the driver's seat. I awkwardly slide into the passenger seat, still not knowing what is happening, and soon we are flying out of the parking lot and zooming down the road.

Maddy speeds down the one major road in our town with her eyes forward, unmoving and uncaring. I sit there nervously, barely breathing, wondering what's going to happen, the car's walls feeling like they're caving in on me.

After a while Maddy's body relaxes and she finally speaks up. "Sorry about all that, just dragging you away."

I lean back in the seat, trying to give off a nonchalant attitude. "It's cool, no problemo." *Shit, that was so weird.*

Maddy must enjoy my weirdness since she laughs. "Yeah, sorry I sort of kidnapped you there, it's a long story."

My eyebrows raise in curiosity, "I mean, we have an hour, right?"

Maddy looks at me and flashes a smile, shaking her head and sighing. "I guess we do have an hour."

Maddy begins to explain the events which occurred after the night of the bonfire. "So Sarah is this sophomore that joined the team this year. I remember her from last year since she kept eyeing Zach. I tried warning her to stay away from him… I even…" She hesitates and takes a deep breath. "Okay, so like, don't judge me on this but I sort of had her do all the clean-up work after practices and made her do extra laps and stuff, but she wasn't listening to me and I needed her to know that I was not okay with her giving all those flirty eyes to Zach!" She pauses, waiting to see how I respond.

"Yeah, I mean, I'm not going to judge you on that, we sometimes do bad things when we're upset. I don't think someone should hold a grudge over you or anything." I'm speaking my honest feelings but I try not to overstep my boundaries. I do believe that she was only acting out because she was upset. She clearly knew Zach was going to try something with that girl, and she also knew she wouldn't be able to stop Zach, so instead she tried to stop the girl.

"Anway, that clearly didn't work…" Maddy begins to go on a nonstop rant about the story. "So, they hooked up on the night of the bonfire, and on Monday, he was for some reason mad at me for disappearing? Like, ugh, but yeah he 'broke up' with me, but at this point I'm used to it, like, he dumps me, goes after another girl, and then comes back to me when he's bored. So we broke up and he's hanging all over Sarah and I'm just sucking it up and waiting like I usually do, but the more we were apart the more I was thinking about how shitty this feeling is." Maddy now shifts to a tone like she's just had an epiphany. "Like, I was lying in bed at night, anxious about when Zach would come back to me. I felt horrible and miserable and my stomach felt like it was rotting, and I started to think, why am I putting myself through this torture? And then I thought about Zach and how he probably never feels this way. He's out there living his best life with Sarah while I'm wallowing in self-pity? Like, that's not fair!" She pauses, waiting for my response.

"Yeah, totally not fair." I start getting excited, hoping that Maddy is finally ready to break free from Zach.

"Anyway, so today at lunch he did his whole 'I miss you, baby, you're the only one for me!' spiel and I honestly had enough."

I sit at the edge of my seat…is this it, did she reject him?

"So I decided to get revenge; two can play at this game." I feel a wave of disappointment crushing me. I had hoped Maddy had given up on Zach, but I also know it's not something you can do overnight.

"He always flirts with other girls when we're together, So, I thought I would do the same." She gets quiet after that, probably so the words can sink in for me. *She's using me to make Zach jealous.* She speaks up again but softer this time. "I'm sorry for choosing you, but you are the only person I can trust."

I take a while to respond. On one hand I am definitely disappointed that she's just using me as a tool to get back at Zach. I'm not mad about being used, but more that she is still trying to hang on to Zach. On the other hand, I hope this makes Zach feel hurt; he should have to go through what Maddy has gone through! It also pains me to know I, someone she has only known for three weeks, am the one she trusts the most.

I finally make my decision on the matter. "If you want to use me to get back at Zach…then you can use me all you want."

Maddy's eyebrows raise. "Really?"

I can tell by her shocked tone that she wasn't expecting that response. "Yeah, I mean, Zach's a prick. If you wanna torture him, I'm all for it." I'm willing to let Maddy use me, but I'm still upset about it, so I work up my courage and decide to punish her a little bit. I angle my body towards her and give a flirtatious smile. "And who knows, maybe I will steal you away from him; you may end up falling for my charms." I wait until she looks at me before giving her a prominent wink.

She lets a quick laugh explode from her, a short "Ha!" before covering her mouth in embarrassment. "I, uhh…" Maddy fumbles with her words through a smile as she tries to come up with a response. *Sorry, Maddy, but you made me upset so I wanted to punish you a bit.* "Jeez, just when I think I have you figured out, you go and throw a line like that out!"

"What can I say? I live life on the edge."

Chapter 12

In no time our hour-long car ride ends and we arrive in a small town. Well, small to my point of view, but much larger than the small town the Owens live in. She pulls into the parking lot for a small mall.

"You ever go to the mall?"

"Only the second largest mall in America." Her eyebrow raises in curiosity as she pulls into a spot. "The King of Prussia Mall…it's like half an hour from me."

"Ugh, lucky, there's nothing around here."

Maddy walks ahead and we talk as I catch up to her steps. "Have you ever thought about moving somewhere else? Like, at least a place where you don't have to drive an hour to get to a mall with three stores?"

"Hey, this mall has more than three stores…it has like ten stores."

I laugh. "Oh right, of course, sorry."

"Of course, I would like to move away somewhere, but it's not that easy."

I hesitate, pondering what she means exactly by "not that easy." Is it a money thing, is it a confidence thing? I yearn for the answers. "Where would you want to go?"

She tilts her head as she thinks for a moment. "Hmm, I know it's a little basic but I would love to live in New York City. I could work at a fashion magazine company like in *The Devil Wears Prada*." She looks down and smiles, reminiscing about her past dreams.

"New York would be tough to move to, but I know you have a 4.0 GPA and you take AP classes! You could easily get into a school in New York!" She laughs; it wasn't the response I expecting. Am I wrong about her having good grades? Or maybe she's like me and doesn't want to go to college. If that's the case I feel bad for bringing it up, I don't want to pressure her or anything. "Sorry, did I say something stupid again?"

"No, it's just…you're going to get mad at me again." Her cheeks flush; it's probably something she's embarrassed about.

"I'm not going to get mad at you." I try to sound reassuring.

She exhales. "Okay, well, the reason I work so hard for good for grades is…" She hesitates, her lips pursed and eyebrows furrowed. "Zach has a sport scholarship for Ohio State… so I study hard so I could also get into Ohio State."

She scrunches up her face, waiting for me to explode at her, but I can't. Although I couldn't stop my eyes from rolling. "You probably already know what I'm going to say…"

"Yeah I know…"

"You should just do what *you* want."

"I know, but I always thought that what I wanted was to be with Zach!" I can tell this worries Maddy. She hides her anxiety behind a forced smile and nervous fidgeting.

"You're still young, take your time and figure it out."

"Ha, I'm not young, I'm a senior in high school. I have less than a year to figure it out."

"Take a gap year," I respond with a calm tone over my voice. To me, this is something natural; if you need more time, just take it.

"I can't. I can't just not go to college for a year!"

"Why not? I'm not going at all."

"You're not?" Maddy wears a look of concern and confusion, like she's never considered not going to college was an option.

"College isn't necessary for my chosen profession in life, but I didn't come to this conclusion overnight. It took a lot of time and research. You should take your time to really consider what *you* want to do before making any big decisions."

Maddy goes quiet. I can see her in deep thought, but the longer she's silent, the more a look of sorrow comes across her face. She is probably looking back at her life choices and realizing she hasn't made a lot of choices based on what she wants.

"So, what do you want?"

"I really don't know!"

"No, I mean to eat…" I gesture around at us. We've somehow found our way to the food court. "You don't need to make any big decisions now, you can just start small… What do you want for dinner?"

She examines the limited options we have. "Hmmm, Chinese?"

"Cool, I'm down."

As we sit down with our food, I can tell Maddy is still deep in thought. She almost walks into a trash can on our way to the table. I want to change the topic somehow, or else she could be in her head all night.

"So, this is a fun date, thanks for inviting me." I reach over to her plate and nab a dumpling with my chopsticks. As she looks up to me with her mouth hanging open, I give her a wink.

"Ha, you wish this was a date." Maddy's not backing down. She grabs a piece of chicken from my stir fry.

"Maybe I do, who knows." I reach over and take a large chunk of white rice out of her bowl.

Her mouth hangs open at her defeat. "Ah! How dare you!"

I do a little evil "hehehe" laugh before going back to my own food. "But don't worry, I'm only kidding about all of this. I respect people's sexuality. If you're straight, you're straight... I'm not going to pursue something that's not going to happen."

"What if I'm *not* straight?" She puts an emphasis on "not" meaning, "I could be gay, you don't know that."

"How do *you* know you're not straight?" I put an emphasis as "you" meaning, "Do you even know if you're gay or not?"

Surprisingly she has to think before answering. "I...I don't know...I've never actually thought about it before. How did you know?"

I am taken aback by the question. I didn't think she would ever be curious about me, especially about my sexuality, but here she is asking me. I want to be as honest as possible with her, so I tell her everything. "Well...I guess I never found myself attracted to boys. All the girls in my class would talk about which boys they thought were the cutest and I just, there were no boys in my class I thought were 'cute.' When I thought about it there were no boys anywhere I thought were cute, but there were girls. I could name all the girls in my class who I thought were cute, who made my heart skip a beat, but I didn't really start to understand until I kissed a girl."

Maddy's eyes are focused on me. She isn't judging me or anything, but she seems like she's trying to understand me.

"I was in the fifth grade. It was during a Girl Scouts retreat. Me and this other girl in my troupe were curious about what it would be like to kiss a girl...so we did. I ended up enjoying it, but she did not. And then I kissed a boy."

"And you hated it?

"And I hated it. We were in seventh grade playing spin the bottle. It was a small kiss but it made my skin crawl. Anyway, what really sealed the deal was when I kissed my best friend in middle school. We were having a sleepover, and I asked if she'd ever thought about kissing a girl. She said no, and…I probably shouldn't have but I asked if she wanted to try… I got more into it than her and that's when I knew, but that's also when she knew…and when she knew she let everyone know, and I became an outcast. The 'dirty dyke' that no one wanted to get near."

Her brows furrow again, a look of pity in her eyes. It isn't something I need. I've come to terms with how I was treated back then and have moved on. The reason I don't open up about this is due to the fact that I don't want pity.

"I'm sorry about that time I called you…*that*."

"Dyke? You don't have to tiptoe around the word, I've heard it more than enough times." I feel myself become annoyed. I don't like when people feel bad for me, I don't like when they try to baby me.

"Still…" As annoyed as I'm getting, I can't deal with seeing my goddess looking upset.

"Look, you were just really upset and angry at Zach, so you took your anger out on me. Meanwhile I've met people who will call me dyke or whatever just because that's how they truly see me. You're not the same."

Things go silent, a long awkward silence. This is why I prefer not to talk about my past, but for some reason, I wanted to tell her, I wanted her to know. But now I'm second guessing if I should have shared.

Maddy shoots up from her seat, and I'm taken aback by the sudden movement. "Let's do some shopping!" She has eagerness in her eyes, begging me to join her.

I'm unsure why there's a sudden change, but there's a sense of urgency in her tone and I'm not going to question it. I simply follow her through the mall.

We go from store to store, trying on outfits and sharing fashion tips. We laugh as we try on different sunglasses, striking poses in front of the store mirror, each outrageous pair adding a touch of whimsy to our shopping adventure. At the end of our shopping spree, we collapse in the car with only one bag each. The only thing I ended up buying was a new dress, a long sleeve floral patterned tan dress that goes to my ankles. I liked how flowy it felt, allowing a gentle breeze to flirt with the fabric as I moved, creating a sense of effortless elegance.

We begin our drive home, the awkward silence gone, instead filled by the sound of laughter. I think I understand now why she wanted to do some shopping; she understood the way I felt, the way I hated the silence, so she wanted a change of pace, something fun we would both enjoy. She really is too good for that asshole Zach.

"You know…" Maddy starts a new conversation. "You don't really dress like a…like how I thought you would."

I smirk. "You mean like a lesbian?"

She has a pinch of panic in her voice. "No! I didn't say…"

I think the panic is cute so I decide to tease her a little more. "Were you expecting short hair…cargo shorts with sneakers?"

Her face goes red. "No!"

I laugh at her embarrassment. "Well, I guess I could say you don't really dress like the popular head cheerleader. I wasn't expecting a leather jacket."

She comically gasps. "How dare you make assumptions about my kind."

Our laughter erupts like a symphony, a harmonious blend of shared amusement echoing through the car. I never imagined I would be able to joke with Maddy like this. I'm used to just watching from afar, knowing that it'll be an unrequited love forever, but here I am, sitting and laughing with her.

It's around nine when we arrive at the Owens's house. The moon is high in the sky and the world quiet.

As I am getting out of the car Maddy calls to me, "Hey, sorry about taking you like that…"

"No, it's okay, I had a lot of fun." This is my genuine answer.

"I know but…now I'm worried about what Zach will do when you get inside."

I laugh it off. "Ha, please, Zach doesn't scare me, and besides, Sam and Charlie have my back. I'll be okay." Even though I say that Maddy still looks concerned. "I mean, if you're that worried you could always come inside and keep me company. You'll love my bedroom. And my bed." I do a goofy wink and Maddy rolls her eyes.

"Okay, whatever… Just try to stay safe." She rolls up her window and heads off with a wave. I wait until her car is out of sight. I want to take in this moment as long as possible, to live in it forever. But things have to come to an end and I go back inside to immediately face Zach in the living room watching football. When he hears the door he shoots up from the couch and rushes over to me, staring me down, but I don't back away. I'm not going to let him intimidate me.

"So, did you have fun with Maddy?"

"I did. Thanks for asking, I enjoyed our *date* a lot." His eyes twitch when I use the word *date*.

He lets out a nervous laugh. "Ha! You really think that was a date?"

I give him a condescending smile. "Maybe it was, you weren't there."

I can tell he's getting angry as his body trembles, but he still tries to play it cool. "She'll never like you, I hope you know what."

"I don't know…" I tilt my head and ask in a sweet voice, "Are you worried I might steal her away from you?"

Zach lets his cool completely fall as he punches the wall next to my head. I do my best not to flinch. "You could never steal her away from me. She's mine."

Hearing that I start to lose my cool, too, and snap at him, "She's not a toy!"

He punches the wall even harder this time, drawing the attention of Sam and Charlie who quickly rush down and put themselves between us.

"Leave her alone, Zach." Charlie stares at him, not blinking once.

"Yeah, just drop it," Sam adds, trying to diffuse the situation.

Zach backs away. "Ha, I can't believe you're siding with her over your own brother."

Charlie steps forward and exhales a laugh. "Please, I haven't considered you my brother for a long time."

Zach raises an eyebrow and smiles. "Oh, you're still not over the time I smashed your little guitar." He has a sense of mockery in his voice that makes Charlie's face get red from anger, his blood boiling with rage. He grabs Zach by the shirt collar and pulls him closer, but Sam pushes him away. Zach smiles as he watches Sam hold Charlie back.

"Come on, he's not worth it." Sam grabs me as he pushes Charlie upstairs and up to my room. Apparently my room is the only one with a lock. Paul put one in after I told him about the boys constantly barging their way into it.

"Damn it!" Charlie hits and kicks the wall. Sam tries to calm him down but I'm content with letting him get his anger out. After a while he starts to calm down, going from heavy breathing to slow, deep breaths. Once I know it's safe, I approach them and pull them both into a hug.

"Thank you for that." Charlie tries to respond but I squeeze the boys tighter. "I don't know what happened between you and Zach, and you don't have to tell me now, but I'll be there to support you just like you were there for me."

I hear a soft "okay" slip from Charlie's mouth and we let go from our embrace. The boys stay up with me as I tell them about my night with Maddy. They listen intently, offering supportive nods and camaraderie, turning that late-night conversation into a cherished memory among friends.

Chapter 13

Maddy's revenge plot takes off after that day. She uses me almost every day to make Zach jealous, running to me as soon as her practice is over and taking me in her car for joyful nights. On the weekends she comes to the house to pick me up, taking me to her "secret spot"—the field we ran through on the night of the bonfire. We are gone for hours and Zach goes mad, but he won't lay a hand on me, not with Sam and Charlie at the house protecting me.

Sam and Charlie spend more time in my room with me. We lock the door so Zach can't enter and talk for hours. They talk about their childhood, how the three of them would compete at everything they did. When they were five they all joined a youth soccer team, but instead of trying to steal the ball from the other team they would try to steal the ball from each other. They eventually start to talk about their mother, what kind of woman she was, how she would wake them up early during the summers to watch the sunrise. How she was known for her unwavering compassion, always lending a listening ear and offering gentle guidance to anyone in need. I wish I could have met her.

Charlie still hasn't opened up about his past with Zach, but I don't mind waiting for a while. Instead he talks about how he got into music, his love for it, how he chose the guitar over the other instruments. His eyes light up as he speaks about the first rock concert he ever went to, how watching The Strokes with his father made him fall in love with the genre.

I also get him to talk about Chloe from time to time.

"I know you like her."

"You don't know that!" His flustered face tells me otherwise.

"It's fine, I won't tell her, that's your job."

"But…" He knows he can't lie to me. "What if she rejects me?"

"Why would she?"

"You did."

I sigh. "Charlie, I rejected you because I'm a lesbian, that's a different case."

"Well! Other girls have rejected me…" He hesitates and gets quiet. "They always pick Zach."

I flinch when I hear Zach's name. Not only has he been hurting Maddy by cheating on her, but the girls he's been cheating with have been girls his brothers like.

"Chloe won't go for Zach, she knows how much of a prick he is."

"I guess but…" He buries his face into his knees. "I don't want to be heartbroken again."

I wish I could just tell him that Chloe has been obsessed over him for years but, one, Chloe asked me not to tell him and I'm a good friend, and two, Charlie needs to build confidence and ask her on his own. If I just tell him he'll know because of me; he needs to realize she likes him on his own.

"What about you, Sam?"

He shrugs. "What about me?"

"I've never heard you talk about a girl you like."

"Oh." He stares off with a blank expression. "I guess there isn't really anyone I like at the moment."

My eyebrows rise at the familiar words, but I don't want to make any assumptions without asking first. "Sam… Could you possibly be…"

"I'm tired so I'm going to head to bed." Sam won't let me finish my question. He probably doesn't want to answer, so instead he waves us off, leaving just me and Charlie.

"Is he gay?" Charlie doesn't sound disgusted or angry, just genuinely curious.

"I don't know…" I don't want to talk about Sam when he isn't here so I try to steer the conversation away. "Just because I'm gay doesn't mean I know when other people are gay."

Charlie purses his lips. "I know what you're doing…" He sighs, giving in. "We don't have to talk about Sam."

I give a small smile. "Thank you."

"Yeah. Yeah, anyway, how are things with Maddy? Are you guys getting any closer?"

To say we're getting closer is an understatement. Maddy and I share everything together, our bond deepened into an inseparable connection. At the mall we try on clothes and shop, but other times we just walk around the shops as Maddy tells me about her love for fashion. She'll point out an outfit on display and comment about how she would fix it. Other times when we're looking at clothes, she will grab me different things to try on saying, "These colors look really good on you," or "I think this matches your aesthetic, try it on!"

I've personally never cared about fashion too much, I just wear clothes I find pretty, but seeing Maddy get so passionate and excited talking about it has sparked a newfound interest within me.

"What made you want to get into fashion?" I ask her one day.

"Hmm, probably the same as most people: fashion magazines." We walk side by side in the mostly empty mall, making me feel like we are the only people in the world.

"Did you read a lot when you were younger?"

"Yeah, my mom would have some laying around the house and I would go through them.

She noticed how interested I was so she would buy me more and even let me watch the New York fashion week on TV."

"Your mom seems like a really awesome person." I try to not let the hint of jealousy show in my voice.

"Yeah, she's a good mother, my father, too. He doesn't really understand my infatuation with fashion, but he supports it."

"Oh." My voice carries a subtle deflated tone, the feeling of inadequacy showing through, but I don't think Maddy picks up on it.

"What about your parents? Do you miss them?"

No, I'm much happier away from them! But I can't say that to her; I don't want her to feel bad about talking about how much she loves her parents.

"I guess a little…"

I guess she picked up on my tone that time, since she never brings up my parents again. I try asking about her parents more, but she gives short answers, probably trying to be considerate of me.

We have our most intimate talks on the field. This is where we discuss our lives, our wants, and our regrets, surrounded by the gentle rustle of grass as if nature itself is a silent confidante to our shared vulnerabilities.

"Why did you start dating Zach?" I finally ask her the question I've been wanting to ask since I first met her.

She doesn't react, just keeps looking up at the sky, watching the clouds go by, as if seeking the answer in the ever-changing pattern. "I guess I just felt I had to."

I raise an eyebrow. "You had to?" I find it hard to believe that that's the true reason.

She lets out a sigh. "I mean, he was the most popular guy at school, I was the most popular girl, it just made sense we would get together. And it's not like I wasn't interested in him at all; he was attractive, every girl wanted him and that included me." I see a look of regret wash over her face. "I felt like, since I was the girl every boy wanted, I was the only girl who was fit for him... I guess I felt entitled to him."

"Hmm..." I'm a little upset she only went out with an asshole like him because she felt obligated to. She goes through all of this torture for nothing.

She senses I'm upset with her answer so she tries to be reassuring. "When we first started dating he was super sweet to me. He'd take me out on dates all the time, tell me how pretty I am. I thought he was the perfect boyfriend."

I contemplate asking her the next question. I don't want to bring up bad memories, but talking things out might be good for her. I take my time formatting the question in my mind. "How long...until things went sour?"

She once again hesitates before answering. I take a look at her face. She doesn't look uncomfortable or upset, she looks calm as if a sense of tranquility has enveloped her features. Like she's coming to terms with how Zach has treated her.

"Six months." She pauses to let that number sink in. "Girls were always throwing themselves at him, I just thought he would reject them since he was with me, but he didn't. For four years he didn't." I can hear pain in her voice when she says the last part. The realization that she has been trapped in a cycle of abuse for four years dawns on her.

The more time we spend together, the more she opens up about her relationship.

"So, what was the plan with college?"

Maddy sits up and stretches. "He wanted me at college with him. At first I thought it was because he loved me and never wanted to be apart from me, but now I'm thinking it's probably so he can keep his eyes on me, make sure no other guy tries to take me away." I snort thinking about how he was worried about *guys* trying to steal her away, meanwhile *I* was in his face threatening to take her away.

Maddy hugs her knees to her chest and gives me a sorrowful smile. "He probably wanted me to be his wife. A good housewife to take care of the children and the housecleaning. A wife he could cheat on for the rest of his life."

"You don't have to be that…"

"I'm not a good person," she spits out abruptly.

"That's not tr—"

She interrupts me again. "No, I am…I'm not a good person."

She won't say why, so I do. "Is it because of the bullying?"

Her eyes widen for a moment before relaxing again. "Oh, so you knew."

"Yeah…" She has a pained expression hidden under a smile, but I can't just ignore what she's done in the past. "My friend Sasha…"

"Sasha Thomas."

"Yeah."

Maddy sighs into her memories. "I remember, it was freshman year. One of the girls on my team was friends with her in middle school. She told me how Sasha liked Zach, and then told me how Sasha was flirting with him, so I tried to make her miserable."

I don't respond. I want to hear everything she had to say.

"A week later that girl ended up dating Zach. She only told me it was Sasha so I wouldn't notice her... I was stupid."

I think long and hard for a while. Maddy isn't stupid. Zach's abuse made her do stupid things. But that doesn't excuse what she's done and how it made people feel. "Do you regret it? The bullying."

She hesitates for a bit. "Yeah...I do... Zach wasn't worth all of the harm I did."

I smile hearing that; my goddess has made a lot of progress. "Well then, if you regret it, then apologize."

"A...apologize?" She acts as if she's never heard the word before.

"Yeah, you know...say you're sorry."

"I...I can't do that!"

"Why not? Is it a sense of pride thing?"

"No! Or...I don't know...I just feel like, even if I apologize, it won't fix anything."

"True...people don't have to forgive you just because you say sorry, but I think by apologizing you're at least admitting that what you did was wrong. Not apologizing is like saying you didn't do anything to warrant an apology...but you said you regret it, right?"

She pouts her lips and looks away from me. "Yeah..."

"Then apologize." I'm calm with my response.

She whips her head to look at me, pleading with her eyes. "I can't!"

I retain my calm. "So it is a pride thing."

"It's not a pride thing! I just...ugh!" I watch as she struggles through her thoughts. As much as I want to, I can't help her with this; she needs to make the decision on her own. "I guess I'm just...scared..."

"What? *The* Maddy Vitis is scared?" I do an overexaggerated gasp.

She frowns. "Don't tease me."

"Okay...I'm sorry... See! It's that easy!"

Maddy rolls her eyes. "Ugh!"

"Okay, okay." I can tell she's struggling through this. "Just like thinking about what you want, you don't have to give a big apology or apologize all at once. You can start small."

She thinks about it for a bit. "I could start by apologizing to Sasha."

"There you go! That's a start."

She once again hides her face behind her knees. "Would you go with me?"

"Tsk, damn, I knew it was a pride thing."

Her head shoots up. "It's not a pride thing!"

Her reaction makes me laugh. "I know, I know. I'm just teasing you...of course I'll go with you. I mean, Sasha's one of my closest friends, I wanna make sure she's okay, too."

Maddy smiles. "Thanks" She lets out a yawn and a stretch and lies down again, resting her head on my lap. I freeze, having a full gay panic. "We should change the topic now." As she looks up at me with her sapphire eyes, my heart starts beating faster and I feel my face blush.

"Umm, yeah." I try looking away from her, not wanting her to see how red my cheeks are. "What do you wanna talk about?"

"Hmm, what's your favorite color?"

I look down at her to see her beautiful eyes blinking with curiosity. "You...you wanna know my favorite color?"

"Yeah? Why not?"

I exhale in a laugh. "Uh, yeah sure, my favorite color is purple, like a dark purple." As I speak, I try not to move, the spot her head is on begins getting hotter.

"Mine is blue, like a pastel blue."

"Oh yeah? I notice you wear that color a lot." I mumble through the words, barely able to think with her on my lap, yet Maddy remains calm.

"Yeah, it's a good color to bring out my eyes." She gently grabs my face and pulls it to look at her. "Don't you agree?"

I can't say anything, my heart is beating so loud I can't even hear my own thoughts. My checks feel as though they are on fire, the warmth spreading rapidly into a deep blush.

Maddy laughs and sits up. "Well, I think that's enough payback."

I am stunned and red from embarrassment. "You!"

Maddy gets up and stretches her legs. "That's what you get for teasing me." She winks and I go even more red.

I start to get up. "Oh, this is not over."

Maddy starts running away. "If you can catch me slow poke!"

"I…" She's right, I am a slow poke, but I still run after her, determined to catch up. The sounds of our footsteps echo as I close the distance, filled by the desire to close the gap between us.

Chapter 14

"Are you ready for this?"

Maddy flips her hair back. "Of course, I'm Maddy Vitis, head cheerleader, honor roll student, and most popular girl in school."

"Alright then, lead the way." I gesture to the lunchroom we're standing in front of. Today is the day Maddy's finally going to say sorry to Sasha after all these years.

I see my friends sitting at a round table to the side of the cafeteria. Sam, Charlie, Chloe, and of course, Sasha.

I look towards Maddy, ready for her to go in, but she stands at the door, legs shaking as she stares at Sasha.

I sigh. "We don't have to do this today if you don't want to."

"No! I need to do this today." I notice how much Maddy is fighting with herself to do this. Apologizing means she's owning up to what she did in the past, but it's also something she feels embarrassed to do. She doesn't like to look back and remember how she treated people, but she also knows she can't move forward from it if she doesn't address it.

I stand by her as she has this battle, waiting for her to make the decision. Finally, she takes one final big breath, and with her body shaking, she enters into the lunchroom.

I follow behind her, but as she is walking slowly I eventually catch up with her, and then I'm leading the way, until we make it to the table.

"Hey, guys."

"Michi! You're here! We were wonde—" Chloe stops as she turns and notices Maddy behind me. Everyone at the table stops and stares at her.

My friends all know how I feel about Maddy, and they say they're all rooting for me, but that doesn't mean they like her. Sam and Charlie know her as the jealous girlfriend to their asshole brother, Chloe knows her as the bitch who bullies her best friend, and Sasha knows her as the girl who made her life miserable freshman year.

They all sit there waiting, I also wait, moving aside to let Maddy through to Sasha. Maddy slowly walks over to her, standing just a few inches away, rubbing her shoulder as she awkwardly avoids eye contact. Sasha turns around in her chair to face her, staring motionless at her.

"Umm…" Maddy finally starts. "Sasha, I wanted to come over here to say…" Her body is shaking as the memories of how she treated her rush back in, but she treks on. "Umm, what I wanted to say is that…" She takes a deep breath. "I'm sorry about what I did to you during freshman year."

Chloe gasps but Sasha remains silent, not showing any emotion. As Maddy goes on talking, she slowly begins to relax, the burden being lifted from her. "I have no excuse for why I treated you that way. I was a jealous idiot that took my anger out on the wrong person and you didn't deserve that. I'm sorry." As Maddy finishes she waits patiently, her eyebrows furrowed as she expects the worst reaction.

The rest of the table withdraws their attention from Maddy and instead focuses on Sasha, also waiting for her reaction.

Sasha's body tenses up for a second as she looks down in thought. We're all on the edge of our seats waiting to see what will happen. After a while her body relaxes and she looks up at Maddy. Maddy tries to fix her posture to show respect to Sasha.

Sasha finally opens her mouth. "Remember in middle school you used to throw those big parties and invite everyone?"

Maddy is taken aback and can't answer. She was prepared for many responses, but this was not one of them.

"Uhh, yeah I remember…" She is cautious with her answer, trying not to anger Sasha at all.

"Those parties were fun, your house is big and you guys always had the best food."

Maddy stands there dumbfounded, not knowing how to respond.

Sasha takes a breath and sighs. "If you throw one of those parties again, and invite everyone, no exclusion, then… I'll forgive you."

Maddy's eyes widen, and as she realizes what Sasha is saying, her face began to lighten. "Yeah, I can do that, just name a date!"

Sasha smiles and nods, pleased with herself. She then turns around and continues eating.

Maddy looks at me, wanting me to praise her. I mouth "good job" and give a hidden thumbs up.

"Wow! A Maddy Vitis party! It's been so long! I should think about what to wear!"

"You would look cute no matter what you wear." Charlie gives a smile to Chloe and she blushes. I'm proud of how much the two have grown more comfortable with each other.

Charlie turns his attention to Sam. "You'll be going, right?"

"Well, if everyone is invited…" He looks towards Maddy who nods. "Then I have no reason not to go, plus I'll probably have to be the designated driver."

Charlie laughs. "Yeah true! You might even end up driving the whole party home!"

The friends all laugh. Even Sam laughs as he rolls his eyes. "God, I hope not."

"It's okay, Sam, I don't really drink much."

"Yeah, Sash, but aren't you the one who got her license suspended from too many speeding tickets?" Chloe points out.

"What? I like getting to places fast. Everyone else is too slow."

The friends all laugh again, joking with each other about who is the worst driver. I notice Maddy still standing there awkwardly, silently enjoying the conversation.

"Do you wanna sit?" I motion to Maddy to take a seat.

She begins to step back. "Oh no, I couldn't."

"You can join us, I don't mind." Sasha is the first to speak up. She barely gives any attention to anyone, just focusing on her stale slice of pizza.

Chloe looks at Maddy with bright eyes, the same eyes she showed me when we first met. "Yeah, come sit! There's no need for you to just stand there! Right, guys?"

Charlie agrees with Chloe. "Yeah, I'm fine with it."

Sam shrugs. "Doesn't bother me."

I smile and address Maddy. "Well, there you go! Come on, have a seat!"

"Okay then." Maddy slowly sits down, putting her lunch box on the table and hesitantly opening it and taking out the contents, as if she's expecting us to suddenly kick her out, but we won't.

"You should do a Halloween party." While concentrating on her lunch, Sasha once again is the first to speak up.

"Oooh! That would be so cool! With all of the spooky decorations!" Chloe starts to get excited.

Maddy is still cautious at the table. "Umm, yeah, that would be cool."

The group starts raving about Halloween costumes and such. Chloe gets Maddy to open up about what she would be, while Charlie adds in group ideas we could do.

"By the way…" Sasha leans in close to me. I thought she was about to say something about Maddy but instead she asks, "The deadline is coming up for the art exhibit, did you finish?"

I nod while taking a gulp of water. "Yeah, I finished over the weekend. I was actually going to talk to Ms. Park about it today during…"

"Ummm, Maddy, what are you doing?" We all turn to face the uptight-sounding voice. It's one of the girls from the cheerleading team, someone I've seen Maddy with from time to time. She's standing with about 3 other girls from the team.

"Oh, Wendy, what are…"

Wendy puts up her hand, interrupting Maddy. "Why are you sitting with these losers? Especially that one…" Her head nods to me. "You don't want people to make up rumors about you." She acts concerned but her tone screams mockery.

I roll my eyes and ignore her comment. Maddy tries to speak up again but Wendy interrupts her. "Honestly Maddy, I don't know what's up with you. You've been ignoring us, not focusing during practice, and you know, Zach says he's worried about you. He says you've been avoiding him to hang out with… her." She once again nods her head towards me.

Charlie and Sam stand up from their seats, ready to defend. "Hey, you can't..."

But the girl interrupts them. "Look, I'm just looking out for Maddy. We're her friends and we want to make sure she's safe."

"Ha..." Maddy gets up slowly, looking like she's finally had enough. "Friends?"

The girl has a disgusted look on her face. "Yeah, your friends."

"When have you ever been my friends?"

The girls all exchange looks with each other. "Uh, we have always looked after you!" She looks offended by Maddy's statement. "How dare you..."

"By sleeping with my boyfriend?" Wendy goes silent and the other girls look away in embarrassment, but Maddy doesn't stop. "Would a friend sleep with another friend's boyfriend?"

"Zach was the one who approached us first!" one of the other girls speaks up, trying to defend the group.

Maddy's voice starts to raise with sadness in it. "Then you should have said no! If you were my friend, you would have been on my side, not his!"

The girls are silent at first, not knowing what to say, but Wendy steps forward. "Why are you acting all innocent in this? You were the one who went around bullying other girls who got close to him. Like, what about Rebecca?" Wendy grabs the arm of one of the other girls and pushes her forward. "She's still hurt about the time you poured juice all over her and ruined her new dress."

Maddy has a hurt expression on her face. "You're right. I'm a bully. I let out my anger and frustration on people that didn't deserve it and it wasn't right. But you were right there behind me. You were always laughing with me and telling me lies." Wendy doesn't answer, so Maddy raises her voice again, this time drawing the attention of everyone in the room. "You were my friend! You should have cursed me out for being a bitch not join me! A real friend would have wanted me to change and be a better person! You should have…" Maddy's body begins to shake as tears start forming in her eyes. I spring up from my seat and go to Maddy's side, unable to stand seeing her up there crying alone. "I'm sorry, Rebecca, I'm sorry! I'm sorry to all of you for how I treated you!" Maddy's shaking voice tells me this was not how she wanted her apology to go. She wanted to give a genuine apology, not one covered in tears.

Wendy eventually clears her throat. "Well, I guess if you finally apologized then…"

"What about you?" Maddy says through her tears.

"What?" Wendy's head twitches in confusion.

"What about my apology? Aren't you going to apologize to me?" Maddy's tears begin to disappear, as anger washes over her face.

Wendy laughs to herself. "Please, what do I have to apologize for? I did nothing wrong."

Something must have snapped in Maddy. All the shaking and anger stops, her body falls into a calm state, replaced by an eerie stillness. "You were never my friend, were you?" She stares at Wendy waiting for her response, but as she stumbles trying to say something, Maddy simply turns around and leaves. Only the clicking of her heels can be heard.

I have nothing to say to the group of girls who made my Goddess cry. They don't even seem to care, so I'm not wasting my breath on them. I simply turn to go after Maddy. Behind me I can hear Wendy say, "Can you believe her?" But then I hear Chloe's voice.

"You guys are bad friends…and bad people!" I hear footsteps approaching behind me as Chloe and Sasha appear on either side of me. "Come on, let's go support our friend." I smile hearing this. I'm no longer going to be the only person supporting Maddy, and it warms my heart to witness the growing network of support around her.

We eventually find Maddy hiding in the same bathroom I found her crying in so long ago, but this time she isn't crying. She's sitting on the ground with her knees pulled to her chest, gently pulling on the string hanging from her ripped jeans with a blank stare.

"Hi." I get down next to her but she doesn't look at me. I look towards Sasha and Chloe who sit down with me. Chloe is about to open her mouth and say something but I put my hand up shushing her; this is one of those moments where you don't want to hear anything, you just want to be heard.

"I guess I never had any friends."

"That's not tru—" Sasha and I put our hands over Chloe's mouth until she calms down. I can tell simply listening isn't something Chloe is used to.

We wait to see what will happen, but Maddy has no response.

It's eventually Sasha who says, "Are you upset?" Sasha speaks in a serious tone. She's not trying to mock or anything, it's a genuine question. Although Maddy had a huge fight with her "friends," she doesn't look upset. She doesn't have any emotion on her face, just a blank stare.

"I'm not upset…but just…" She sighs, trying to figure out the feeling. "Surprised? But I guess not since they really never treated me like a friend. Disappointed, maybe? Disappointed in them…disappointed in myself… I don't know, I'm just trying to process."

Chloe tries opening her mouth again but I speak over her. "You can have all the time you need to process things, okay?"

She sighs and looks up at Sasha "Sasha I'm so sorry about how I treated you. I really am. You did not deserve what I did to you." Maddy's voice shakes "I'm so sorry."

Sasha does not respond right away. She nods for a bit before adding "If you ever try to bully anyone ever again I will personally slap that glittery eye shadow off your face." Sasha gives me a smile.

Maddy smiles as she understands

Chloe is finally able to get her opinion heard. " we'll be here to support you! You can sit with us at lunch, and oh! Oh my god, the group Halloween costume!"

"Chlo, you're saying too much again."

"Yeah, because you and Michi kept cutting me off!"

"Yeah… because you say too much!"

Chloe and Sasha start going back and forth, but their arguing makes Maddy smile.

While the two are at it Maddy addresses just me. "I feel like you're always giving me time."

"Hmm?"

"Time to decide what I want to do in life, time to process things…you may end up waiting for a while."

"If it's you I don't mind waiting." Both Maddy and I freeze as we realize what I just said. "Sorry…I…I didn't mean for that to come off as weird as it did…"

Maddy's eyes are wide and a flush of pink comes across her cheeks. Soon her beaming smile comes back and her infectious laughter fills the room, stopping Sasha and Chloe's fight.

Maddy pulls me into a hug and I don't move a bit. "Is…this…are you trying to mess with me again?"

She holds me tight and nuzzles her head into my shoulder blade. "No…I just needed this."

Say less, my queen. I wrap my arms around her back , embracing the warmth of the moment. "Anytime." *I would wait a lifetime for you.*

Chapter 15

"Michelle." Ms. Park pokes her head up over her pile of papers.

"Yes?" I make my way over to the tired-looking teacher.

"I got a call from the Dayton Museum."

"Really? Already? Did my piece get picked?"

Her narrowed eyes look at me for a while, dread starting to form as I think about the possibility of a rejection.

"They called to inform me that they have safely received your piece." My body relaxes a bit, but now I have to go back to waiting.

"Do you know when we'll find out if my piece was picked…or not picked?" I don't want to think about the possibility that it won't be picked.

"The curators received your number and info when you submitted your work. They'll call you when they make a decision…probably."

I probably should be used to Ms. Park's noncaring attitude, but I've been stressing over this since we submitted it a week ago.

While walking with Sam and Charlie to the car, I voice all of my anxieties. "Liked she didn't even say if my piece looked good or anything! She saw it and was like, 'Is this the piece?' I'm like, yeah? And she just nodded. And that was it! Like, no, 'Oh this is good,' or, 'Maybe add a little more blue to this part.' I got nothing! It makes me feel like my piece wasn't good at all."

"Well…you've been working on this since you first came here, and I swear when you get into painting I'm not able to reach you for a while," Sam says as he tries to comfort me.

"True, remember that time we were running late for a reservation and we were knocking on her door for an hour?"

"Oh my god, Charlie, don't bring that up…"

But as always Charlie doesn't listen and goes on laughing, "We had to skim the wall and climb into your room! And you still didn't respond!"

"Ugh, don't remind me."

"Yeah, even when we fell into your room, you didn't look up!

"Sam, not you, too!"

Charlie continues the story, laughing. "And then Dad tried to get in but fell off the roof…"

Sam piggybacks off of Charlie, "And then we ended up having to go to the hospital and missing the reservation…"

Charlie finishes the story, "And then Zach ran off with the car and we were stuck at the hospital until we got a ride from our neighbor. Good times, good times."

My face is bright red. "Okay, okay, I get it, I get into my work! But that's why Paul now has a key to my room."

Sam tussles my hair. "We're just trying to say that you worked really hard on this painting, and they'd be blind if they didn't pick yours."

Sam and Charlie do their best to comfort me, but I just can't get rid of this pained feeling in the pit of my stomach. The anxiety building up and I can barely keep my mind on anything else.

We make our way to the car, but I am so in my head I don't even notice Zach standing there asking where Maddy is.

"Well, is she avoiding you, too?"

I look up at him puzzled, my mind a million different places. "What?"

"I'm saying I don't see Maddy around. Did she finally get bored of you?"

I roll my eyes and push past him. "She wouldn't get bored and ditch someone, she's not you. Also she has a big test coming up tomorrow so she's going home to study."

"What did you say about me?" I can feel Zach walking up to me but I am too concerned about the art exhibit to deal with him so I just get into the car.

As we drive home my head keeps spinning. My chest tightens, breaths becoming shallow as an unsettling wave of anxiety washes over me. Restless thoughts race, each one contributing to the growing sense of unease that knots my stomach.

I think during the ride Charlie tries to say something to me but I don't even register it. As we get in, Zach ran runs ahead of us all, ignoring us as usual. I feel like a zombie moving through rooms of the house. As I'm trying to do housework, I keep walking into walls and tripping over laundry baskets, so even Paul notices something's up.

"Michelle, is something wrong?" Paul is able to sound both chipper but worried at the same time.

"I'm just tired.,,"

"Are you having trouble sleeping?"

"Yeah, I guess."

Paul grabs the laundry basket out of my hands. "Well, then this can wait! You go upstairs and rest, okay?"

"No, Paul, it's fine, I can work."

"Upstairs!" Paul points upstairs with a stricter appearance, but I can't help but laugh at how out of character he's being.

"Okay, okay." I appreciate Paul's kindness but the work was keeping my mind off the art exhibit, so now I'll go upstairs and worry some more.

"Psst, Michelle." I look over to see Sam beckoning me with his hand from his door.

I hesitantly walk over. "What?"

"Come in, I wanna show you something."

I slowly step forward. "You've never invited me into your room before." As I walk in, I'm not surprised at all. His room is exactly what I thought it would look like, filled with a mix of creativity and order. His shelves are lined with textbooks, sci-fi stories, and a few books on woodwork. A well-used desk showcases a laptop and study materials, reflecting a balance between leisure and responsibility.

The most remarkable thing about his room is the furniture; everything yells a Sam Owens original. The smooth texture with a finishing shine, all things Sam's work is known for.

He motions me to sit on his navy blue sheeted bed that matches his navy blue walls. I take a seat, trying not to wrinkle the covers. "So, what's up?"

He grabs his laptop and sits next to me on the bed, hurriedly opening the laptop with excitement reaching off his fingertips. "Look."

What I see is a website, a cute-looking website full of warm colors and the words "Sam's Symmetry" written on it. The first photo I see on the website is a chair. It has a sculpted design, with gracefully curved backrest and intricately carved details. I recognize it as one Sam made. As I go through the album, they all feature professional-looking pictures of Sam's work.

"Sam…is this?"

"My website...to sell my furniture."

"Sam, this is!" As I look at the website, a proud smile slowly forms on my lips, my chest swelling with a sense of accomplishment. "You..." I shake my head in disbelief. I have no words to express how happy I am for him.

"I thought about what you...about how I should start my own business...and seeing how much work you put into your painting and how much you want it to make it to a gallery. I decided, why not at least try? So I made this website."

"Sam!" Wrapping my arms around his neck, I pull him in for a hug, the excitement bursting out of me.

I think I'm hugging a little too tight so he pushes me off. "Hold on, don't celebrate too soon, this is just to see...if I can actually pursue woodwork as a profession. If I can't sell anything in the first week then..."

I put my hand on his. "Hey...this is a start. I'm glad you made this. And someone will definitely buy something!"

He smiles. "Also now you don't have to be the only person nervously waiting for something. I am also waiting to see if I get a request."

I narrow my eyes. "Is part of the reason you made this so I wouldn't have to stress alone?"

Sam looks away. "Maybe..."

"Sam!" I playfully push him over. Although not the best reason to pursue your passion, I'm too happy to stop smiling.

The moment is interrupted when the door opens, but it's just Paul. "Hey, Sam, we're running low on groceries, run over and pick some up, okay?"

"Uh, yeah, of course."

"Also, we need some help in the warehouse if you're free this weekend."

"Okay." Sam smiles but it isn't genuine. There's a hint of sadness in his eyes.

"Paul, I can go to the grocery store." I want to recommend myself. I've noticed whenever Paul needs something, like setting the table or running errands, he always asks Sam. Sam will always say yes, but his eyes drop down and his smile curls.

"That's okay, Michelle! You go upstairs and rest!" *Damn it, Paul, stop being so nice.* I don't want Sam to go out—he clearly doesn't want to go but he doesn't know how to say no.

"Well, actually, Paul…" I try to think of an excuse. "I have a test tomorrow and Sam is helping me study for it. I've been really worried about it! Maybe one of the other boys could go?"

Paul tilts his head while considering the offer. "Alright, fair enough." A faint smile plays on his lips as he leaves. We hear his footsteps land in front of Charlie's room.

Sam tries speaking up, "Why did…"

"Why don't you tell Paul you don't like taking on all of the responsibilities?"

Sam quiets with an embarrassed look. "Well…I am the oldest."

I get frustrated after hearing that. "Oldest by like, what, five minutes? You're all eighteen, you can handle the same stuff!"

"Yeah, but I've been taking on the responsibilities for so long that's it's become second nature to me. I guess I'm used to it."

I start heating up, the frustration boiling in me. "Being used to something and being happy are *very* different, you know that, right?" I know I'm being harsh but Sam is so close to becoming his own person, to making his own decisions, I just need to push him a little more.

Sam shakes his head. "Dad relies on me."

"He has two other sons who can help him." I'm getting too heated, so I take a breath and try a more reassuring approach. "Paul's a great guy, he'll understand."

Sam wears a broken smile. "He's not as good as you think."

This makes me very angry. Paul is a kind soul and there are *way* worse parents…but to Sam, Paul isn't the nicest father, and I have to respect that.

"My father never supported me."

This piques Sam's interest. "Really?"

I sigh, not wanting to think about it, but Sam, I want him to hear my story.

"He said painting isn't a real job, that it's just a hobby that's taking time away from me learning a real skill. One of the reasons I sell or donate a lot of my paintings is because if my Father saw them in the house, he would destroy them. I used to hide all of my art supplies under my bed and only paint outside the house."

"What about your mom?"

"My mom didn't mind me painting, but she couldn't stand up to my father. Although…" A soft smile finds its way to my mouth as I remember a fond memory. "She would always sneak me paints and canvases without my father knowing."

"I'm…" Sam runs his fingers through his hair while his face contorts, probably processing what I just said. Eventually he relaxes. "I guess my situation sounds a lot better than what you went through."

"To me, yeah." I'm direct with Sam, which prompts a defeated smile from him. "But to you, your situation is hard. Don't compare yourself to me."

"I guess..."

"What I'm trying to get at is, Paul might be a lot more understanding than you think, you just need to be honest with him." Sam chuckles "What?" I'm somewhat offended that he think my heartfelt speech is amusing.

"It's just…you sounded like my mother."

"In a good way or a bad way?"

He smiles more. "A good way. I miss my mother a lot. She always tried to support me and gave the best advice. I felt like she had the answers to everything."

"I wish I could have met her."

He smiles, reminiscing. "She would have loved you, especially the way you speak up to Zach. She would have liked your confidence."

Thinking about the boys' mother makes me smile. I like to imagine her slapping at Zach's and Charlie's hands as they fight over food in the morning and scolding them. I imagine her being the loudest at Zach's football games and loudly gloating about Sam's woodwork. I could also see her taking Charlie to music lessons and brushing his curly hair. If she was a woman who could deal with these three boys, then she must have been incredible.

I smile. "I guess that makes me the official mom friend of the group." I stand up and dust myself off. I disappear from Sam's room, leaving him confused for only a second until I return with the laundry basket. I raise my head and deepen my voice to try to sound mature.

"Okay, Sam, I'm doing laundry now, so gather all of your dirty clothes."

Sam laughs. "What are you doing?"

I drop the act. "I'm being the mom of the group." I raise my head and get back into the mom character. "Ehhem, laundry, Sam…" He shakes his head while laughing and throws in his dirty laundry at me.

"Now then, make sure you brush your teeth before going to bed, and oh, make sure you talk to your dad…" I drop the mom act. "He'll listen to you…he loves you three, even though you can all be crazy sometimes."

"How am I crazy?"

I stop to think for a moment before remembering something. "When you're making something, you get this crazy look in your eye."

Sam's eyebrows furrow. "Crazy look?"

"Okay, I gotta work, bye!" I shut the door on a confused-looking Sam, but open it back up to say one more thing. "Keep me posted about the website, okay?"

Sam smiles. "I will."

As I close the door I realize something. The whole time with Sam, I hadn't thought of the art exhibit. I laugh to myself. "Sam, you really…" Here I was thinking I was helping Sam, but the whole time he was helping me. "That's no fair…" I mumble under my breath.

Sam helped me calm down and get my mind off of the exhibit, so now it's my turn to do something for Sam. I walk over to Paul's room and knock on the door. I hear a "Come in!" So I enter.

"Oh, Michelle!" Paul is in bed reading a book. I never thought of Paul as someone who reads before bed, yet here he is. He notices my laundry basket. "You don't have to be doing chores today! You aren't feeling too well, and you have that test, don't you?"

I smile as I begin dumping Paul's laundry into my basket. "I'm feeling better now, and Sam helped me study for the test. He's very smart and helpful."

Paul smiles. "He's a really great kid, my oldest, the one I can count on for anything."

"But maybe you count on him a little too much?" I pause after I say that, feeling nervous that Paul might get mad at me for speaking up.

But he cocks his head in confusion. "I don't think I do…"

He doesn't get angry so I push it a little more. "Have you asked Sam how he feels about it? About taking on a lot of responsibilities?"

"Well, of course! When he was younger, he would always be eager to help me out!"

I start to understand a little. Sam was excited to help his father out when he was younger, but as he got older he kind of got stuck, and his father still thinks Sam's okay with it.

"Have you asked Sam recently?"

"I…" Paul pauses. Probably because he realizes that he hasn't asked Sam in a while.

I grab my laundry basket and begin to head out, but I need to say one more thing. "Paul I…I don't have a good relationship with my father."

He looks shocked by what I say at first, but eventually looks down. "Yeah, I had figured it was something like that."

"My father has these high expectations of me, and when I try to tell him he doesn't listen." Paul sits there, looking down and nodding, probably understanding what I'm inferring. "I don't think you want your sons to grow distant from you."

Paul closes his book and frowns. I fear I might have said too much so I bid him a "good night." And leave.

Paul's not a bad guy, I think there was just a misunderstanding, and I trust Paul to make the right decision.

***

The next morning I'm worried Paul will be upset with me, so I head downstairs slowly. If I'm going to be berated by Paul I would like to delay it as much as possible. As I get closer down the stairs, I can hear Paul whistling as he cooks, and I feel a little relieved. *At least he's not in an awful mood.*

"Move, you're walking too slow…" Zach pushes past me on the stairs, almost knocking me down.

"Prick!"

"Who, me?" I turn around and see Sam coming down the stairs next.

I narrow my eyes and shoot him a "Seriously?" glance. He smiles and catches up to me.

We walked into the dining room together where Zach and Charlie are already sitting.

"Wow, I actually beat Michelle down here? Wild."

I roll my eyes at Charlie. "I had a long night."

We hear Paul finish up in the kitchen and then hear his voice call out, "Zach, come in here and help carry the dishes."

Zach's brows furrow and a frown appears on his lips. "Why? Just ask Sam to do it!" Both Sam and I stare in disbelief at Zach's comment; this guy is really like a toddler.

Paul shouts back, "Sam helped me yesterday, and the day before. I want you to help me today." Paul is more firm this time. Zach knows he can't reject his father.

He scoffs and huffs as he gets up. "Ugh, fine!" He disappears into the kitchen.

Sam's eyes widen with a bewildered look on his face. I nudge him and smile. Sam's eyes widen at me; he must have figured I said something.

Paul walks in with Zach carrying a bunch of plates. As he sits down and the breakfast match begins, Paul addresses Sam. "You know, Sam, we don't need help anymore at the warehouse this weekend. So you don't have to worry about that." Sam's eyes look up at Paul. He's shocked and doesn't know what to say. Paul continues, "And if there's anything else you want to do, let me know. You kids are grown ups now, old enough to make your own decisions." Paul motions towards Charlie and Zach, "That goes for you two, too." Charlie nods in confusion and Zach doesn't respond, but Sam has a wide smile, a smile I haven't seen from him yet.

"Thanks, Dad." Paul smiles, then looks at me and gives me a "Thank you" wink. "Actually, Dad…" Sam continues, "I've made this website…" Sam goes on to tell Paul about his business idea and how much he loves his wood work. Paul sits there smiling and nodding with his son.

I'm glad Paul is so supportive and understanding, but as happy as I am for them, I can't help but feel a pinch of envy.

Chapter 16

"Okay, So I have the perfect idea for our group Halloween costumes!" Chloe has been brainstorming ideas since she found out about the party. She recommends Powerpuff Girls. Sasha and Maddy and Chloe would be the girls, Sam would be the professor, and then Charlie and I would be villains. I shut that down. She thinks about superheroes, Mario Kart, and eventually lands on, "We'll do the crew from Scooby Doo!"

There are no reactions, but that is mostly due to the group not really caring about group costumes.

"I like that idea, the Scooby gang has cute outfits!" Maddy adds, not wanting Chloe to feel embarrassed.

Since the fight with her "friends," Maddy started sitting with us and ingratiating herself into our group. She was a little awkward at first, not knowing how to join into the conversation, but after a while she began to open up.

"You have red hair, so you'll be a good Daphne."

Chloe becomes flustered at Maddy's comment." What? No way! I couldn't be Daphne, I mean you're way prettier, you should be Daphne."

Maddy looks a little embarrassed. "No way…"

"I get to be the dog," I state, not asking, demanding.

Chloe raises her eyebrow. "You want to be the…"

"Yeah, I have this really cute brown dress I've been wanting to wear, I'll just need dog ears and the collar."

"Then I'll be Shaggy!" Maddy adds next, following my lead of demanding not asking. "I've been really into the baggy aesthetic lately, I would love to style an outfit like that. Plus I have long hair." She flips her hair, her fruit-scented shampoo filling the air.

"I guess I'll be Velma since I have the shortest hair." Sasha doesn't really demand, but is more of accepting her role.

I decide to use this chance. "Then Chloe you'll be Daphne and Charlie can be Fred." I want to use this opportunity to have Chloe and Charlie in a couples costume.

I enjoy seeing Chloe's face turn pink. "I, uh…"

Maddy interrupts before she can object. "We should go shopping after school for outfits! I bet I could find you a really cute purple dress!"

I nudge Maddy. "We also need to find something for the boys…"

"Wait, hold on!" We all turned to look at Sam. "Aren't you forgetting someone?"

Chloe goes silent. She doesn't know how to tell him, so I decide to do it for her.

"Well, you know we can't be Mystery Inc. without the Mystery Machine."

I watch as the realization crosses his face. "Wait no…I am not being a stupid van…"

***

I have Sam and Charlie in my room while I paint the cardboard cutouts to look like the Mystery Machine. We take two pieces of cardboard and draw outlines that look like the side of a van. We then add another rectangle piece at the front and back. Lastly we attach elastic to it so that Sam can wear it over his shoulders, and voila, the Mystery Machine.

Sam still isn't pleased with being the van, but I assure him it will be cute and to leave it to me. Thanks to Sam, I've been stressing less about hearing back from the art exhibit. He's been giving me updates on his website and that has been occupying his mind. So far, he's had about

1,000 visitors to the site and a few people have reached out to him about products, but no buyers yet. Paul has also been dividing the housework between the three boys so it's no longer falling only on Sam. I've noticed how much happier Sam has been feeling, but there's still something that concerns me.

A while ago he mentioned how he never felt attractive to girls. I don't know if that means he's gay or not, and I don't know how to bring it up. For now, I'll just observe him and see what I notice.

"I can't believe you made Chloe and I Fred and Daphne!" Charlie says.

"What, that wasn't on purpose or anything, they were the only characters left."

He rolls his eyes. "Yeah, sure."

"You gotta ask her out soon. You guys are basically a couple already, just make it official!"

His face goes red as he scrambles for a response, but he has nothing.

Charlie and Chloe have grown a lot since their first interaction. Now I see them engaging in playful teasing and deep conversations. Sometimes they get so into a conversation that they don't even notice us there. There's also romantic gestures and Charlie will compliment her and help her carry her bags and lunch tray. You can also just tell from the way they look at each other, they have such affection in their eyes. Like they're the only people in the world.

I like to imagine Maddy and I could be like that one day. If Maddy would ever look at me with affectionate eyes. When I have these thoughts I try to think of something else right away. I don't want to have these hopes, only to know they will never come true. I'm content with the relationship we have now, but sometimes, I crave more.

With the party happening the next day, Chloe, Sasha, Maddy, and I drive to the mall to go shopping for the costumes. Maddy is excited to show off her fashion expertise to Chloe and Sasha.

"Did you finish up the car costume?" Chloe asks, walking proudly through the mall next to Maddy. She was excited to go shopping with Maddy because she felt she would look cool.

"Yeah, last night. Charlie helped, too. Sam's still pissed, but it's all for the cause."

"I'll make sure to find stuff for Sam and Charlie." Maddy once again flips her hair confidently, feeling good about her knowledge of fashion.

Maddy does look cool, you can tell she's *that* girl at school, the girl all the boys admire and all the girls are jealous of. She sticks out in our group as well. Me with my modest dresses, Sasha with her blue hair and mismatched clothes, and Chloe wearing just a plain T-shirt and jeans. Maddy looks as though she's glowing.

I feel myself falling for her more and more every day. I keep learning new things about her that make my heart race even more. I know this is bad, I know if I keep liking her my heart is only going to break more, but I can't help myself.

I need to last the rest of the year, I can keep an unrequited love up for that long, and then hopefully Maddy will have her own things she wants to do and we can leave as friends. It'll be hard but I'll try. At least she isn't with that prick anymore. I'm glad I was able to save her a little.

Tomorrow is the Halloween party, and the whole school will be there, including Zach. I just hope it'll end peacefully.

Chapter 17

I put on my brown dress. It's just a simple dress with three-inch straps and a heart-shaped top. I put on a black belt which has a makeshift tail attached to it. I finish off the look with ears bought at a Halloween store and a Scooby Doo collar Maddy made for me.

I was surprised when she said she would make it. "You know how to sew?"

"A little. I don't have my own sewing machine or anything, so I mostly sew rips or buttons. I do want to get into more."

"You're smart, athletic, fashionable, and now you can sew? Is there anything you can't do?"

"Hmmm, date a nice guy?" We both laugh. I'm glad she's at the point where she can joke about it, as it shows she's growing and moving on.

As I finish getting ready I go downstairs to meet Sam and Charlie. Charlie had on basic blue jeans, a white long-sleeve shirt that Maddy stitched blue collar on, and the orange scarf that Fred wears. Sam is reluctantly holding the makeshift Mystery Machine costume.

"You're not going to wear it?"

"I can't drive a car, looking like a car..."

I nod. "Makes sense..." Even though Sam is saying how much he hates the costume, he looks really excited for the party.

As we head downstairs, I look around and listen for Zach. "Where's Zach? I feel like I haven't seen him all day." *Not that I'm complaining.*

"Some of his football friends came and picked him up this morning, who knows what they're doing…" Charlie says as he swings the door open. "If we're lucky maybe they'll skip the party."

I smile. "That would be nice." In an ideal world Zach and his asshole friends won't attend, and we might have a drama free party, but I know that won't be the case. Zach's going, and he's going to try to talk to Maddy. I'll just make sure that doesn't happen.

"Are we picking up Sasha and Chloe or are they getting their own rides?" Sam asks as he gets into the driver's seat.

"They said they'll meet us there."

"Then let's go."

We drive about twenty minutes to get to Maddy's house. Just like the Owens she owns a large property with no other houses in sight. As we arrive at the house, my mouth hangs open. "Holy shit, she lives in a mansion."

Her house has towering spires and intricate architecture, and lush gardens frame the magnificent structure. The sun's golden rays dance on the elegant facade, casting a warm glow on the marble columns and ornate details. As we walk up the white stairs to the front doors, I count twenty jack-o'-lanterns, ten on each side. We knock and Maddy opens the door. My jaw drops again.

Maddy wears an oversized baggy green T-shirt, but instead of looking like a kid in adult clothes, she's fitted it to look trendy. She's tucked the shirt into brown pants that are tight around her waist but baggy down her leg. Her makeup is more of a punk tone than the normal soft tones she does—dark maroon lipstick and black eyeshadow. I want to compliment her, I want to scream about how much she nailed the look and how beautifully detailed the makeup is, but I'm nervous and all I can say is, "Damn girl you look sexy." *Shit.*

Maddy freezes for about a millisecond before bursting out laughing and I am completely mortified. "You look really cute, too, Michelle," Maddy says as she's still laughing. I sigh. I then hear the muffled laughter of Sam and Charlie behind me.

"I swear if you two say a single word…"

Charlie and Sam try even harder to keep their laughs and snickering down.

"I mean, if you want alone time Sam and I can wait in the car…"

I stomp on Charlie's foot to shut him up. "Shall we go inside?"

"Sure." Maddy, still laughing, leads us in. The inside of the house is just as marvelous as the outside.

Upon stepping through the ornate double doors, I find myself in a vast foyer adorned with a sparkling chandelier that cascades light onto a marble floor. The air carries the faint scent of polished wood and antique furniture. Expansive halls branch off, revealing opulent rooms filled with plush furnishings, large family portraits, and gilded accents. Each room holds its own charm, creating a labyrinth of luxury within the grand mansion.

Around the house are small Halloween decorations. There are ghosts hanging from the ceiling and spider webs on tables. A candy bowl with a zombie hand coming out of it is next to the door. The rooms are lit up with orange and purple lights, and a plastic jack-o'-lantern is placed in each of them.

We get there an hour before the party officially starts. We told Maddy we would help her prepare, put drinks in the cooler, get snacks out, set up a playlist, and things like that.

"Are your parents home?" I ask in awe as Maddy leads us through her labyrinth of a house.

"No, they said they didn't want to deal with loud teenagers so they're spending the night with some friends."

"Wow, so your parents just let you have a party? Knowing it'll get wild?" I didn't know this was possible, although I've never been invited to a high school party so what would I know? Usually in movies the kids wait until the parents are out of the house and then throw a massive party.

"Yeah, my parents are cool with it. They said they're proud of how I've been doing in school so this is a reward, I guess."

"Damn, our dad would never..." Charlie says as he spins around, looking at every corner of the room.

Maddy leads us into the kitchen. "If you guys wanna start pouring snacks into bowls I'll go grab the cooler..."

"It might be heavy so let me help you." Good guy Sam runs to follow Maddy. I give death glares to Sam. He meets my eyes and I give him the "are you challenging me?" look. Sam shakes his head in fear, but I put my two fingers to my eyes and do the whole "I'm watching you" movement. Sam and Maddy disappear so it's just me and Charlie.

"So what's your plan?" I ask Charlie in a casual way as I pull open a bag of pretzels.

He shifts his eyes. "What do you mean?"

"With asking Chloe out!"

"Oh my god..." Charlie begins to do a whole head roll.

"I swear if you don't ask her out, I will! And this time I'm not kidding!"

Charlie gets flustered. "Why can't we just stay as friends? Why do you care so much?"

I pout and stand up to face him. "Because I know how much you two like each other and if you like each other you should date! Do you know how painful it is to be friends with someone you like but will never date because you *know* they don't like you back?" I'm obviously talking about myself, and by Charlie looking away from me he's probably figured it out. "You know Chloe likes you!" I feel myself getting worked up so I bring it back a bit. "You two are my friends…I want you to be happy together."

Charlie gets up. "I know, and I get how you feel with an unrequited love." He takes a breath. "The truth is…" He rubs the back of his neck while looking away, meaning whatever he's trying to say is hard to admit. "I've never actually dated anyone before."

He waits to see my shocked reaction, but I'm not shocked at all. "Yeah I know…"

"Wait, how did you know…"

"From the way you act. Clearly you've never dated anyone before."

Charlie hangs his head. "Oh."

"So the reason you've been so hesitant to ask Chloe out is because you don't know what you're doing?" He doesn't say anything, just gives a little nod. I end up chuckling since his behavior reminds me of a little kid. "So what, you don't know what you're doing? I don't know what I'm doing. You saw what I said at the door. I have no idea how to talk to Maddy sometimes! But just because I don't know doesn't mean I don't try!"

The only response I get from Charlie is a little chuckle. He mumbles, "Damn, girl, you look sexy," in a mocking tone under his breath.

"Tsk, and after everything I've tried to do to help you." I playfully turn to leave but he grabs me and pulls me into a back hug.

"Wait wait wait, I'm sorry…I'll talk to Chloe tonight…I'll try to ask her."

I turn around to face him and with a sweet baby voice, I say, "Really?"

He laughs softly and smiles. "Yes, so please don't be mad at me."

"Fine…"

"Oh, are we interrupting something?" I turn to see Maddy standing there with her arms crossed and an annoyed expression on her face.

I quickly distance myself from Charlie. "No, no, we were just talking about Chl…"

"Mmhmm… sure…" She turns around with an overdramatic hair flip and storms to the fridge. Sam appears with the cooler and drops it next to her.

Maddy starts throwing cans of soda into the cooler. I walk over and squat next to her. I tilt my head and ask, "Are you angry?" in a sweet voice.

She turns her head away from me. "No, I'm not angry…"

I get a mischievous grin. "Then are you jealous?"

Maddy scoffs. "Ha! Why would I be jealous?"

I inch myself closer to her. "I don't know, maybe you…"

We're interrupted by the sound of the doorbell. Maddy stands up. "That must be Sasha and Chloe! I'll go let them in." As she hurriedly exits, I swear I see a bit of pink in her cheeks.

"Maybe it's not so unrequited." Charlie startles me by whispering next to my ear.

I jump. "No, she's just teasing me, we do that a lot…"

"I don't know, didn't look that way to me. What do you think, Sam?"

Sam has soft eyes and a worried expression. "Sam, what's wrong?"

"Nothing is wrong with me, but when Maddy and I were alone together she asked about Zach."

My heart sinks. "Oh?" I try to not sound upset.

"She asked if we knew if he was coming to the party, but that was it." Sam tries sounding reassuring. "She could have been asking because she doesn't want him here."

I give him a faint smile, "Yeah probably." I try to stay positive, but this news is a major blow. Underneath my attempt at reassurance, a wave of uncertainty and disappointment lingers.

"Hey, Michi!" Chloe's head appears from around the corner. She comes out in full view with her costume. I enjoy seeing Charlie's mouth fall open. I nudge him and mouth, "You should say, 'damn, girl, you look sexy.'" He pushes me away and says, "Shut up," under his breath.

He nonchalantly walks over to Chloe. She's wearing a short tight purple dress with the iconic neon green scarf around her neck. The purple headband in her hair compliments her red color. "You look very pretty." He tries to sound cool while speaking, but his voice cracks and ruins the moment. Chloe chuckles, the way she looks at him revealing a mix of amusement and affection.

"You don't look too bad yourself, Fred." She teases him with a playful glint in her eyes. He nervously rubs the back of his neck, a common quirk I've seen from him.

"Can y'all stop flirting for a sec?" Sasha emerges from the corner and I scream from shock, quickly covering my mouth to save face. For the costume Sasha's dyed her hair orange. Orange to match the orange turtleneck sweater she's wearing. She has dark orange lipstick that matches the pleated skirt we got her.

"What? Do the glasses look too fake?" She takes off the fake glasses we got at the same store I got my dog ears.

"No, obviously I'm not freaking out about the glasses, but your hair!" I say while motioning to her hair.

"What, is the orange hair somewhat more outrageous than the blue hair?"

"No, it's great!" I feel like everyone's pulling a prank on me; how am I the only one freaking out?

Chloe comes up behind me and puts her hand on my shoulder. "She dyes her hair once every three months or so. You get used to it changing eventually."

"Oh…" I blush, feeling embarrassed about overreacting.

"Hey, don't sweat about it, I should have given you a heads up." Sasha gives me a thumbs-up, but with the condescending smile she's giving, it isn't sincere at all. Sasha claps her hands and looks around. "Shall we set this party up?

We have less than an hour to put out all of the food and fill up the coolers with sodas, water, and of course, alcohol. In no time the doorbell is going off so much we eventually just leave the door open for people to come in and out. The party pulses with vibrant energy as music reverberates through the air, creating a rhythmic heartbeat for the lively gathering. Colorful lights adorn the space, casting a kaleidoscope of hues on the dancing crowd. Laughter and animated conversations echo against the walls, as teens drink and smoke throughout the rooms.

I try to spend the whole night with Maddy, making sure that Zach won't get near her while also keeping eyes on the rest of my friends. Sasha is in the corner gnawing down on some candy; surprisingly Sam is chatting with a cute girl; and to my joy, Charlie is standing with his arm around Chloe as they talked to some other people.

I get close to Maddy's ear so she can hear me. "Look!" I point to Charlie and Chloe.

Maddy covers her mouth in excitement. "Oh my god, Do you think he told her?"

"I friggin' hope so, I've been telling him to do it for the last two weeks!"

Maddy laughs and pulls out two cans. "You ever shotgun a beer?"

I take the can and cheers with Maddy. We punch holes in the sides of the beer cans and drink up.

"Whoo! That was good." I look up to Maddy but her face is frozen, frightened. I look over to what she's looking at and see Zach with his football buddies wearing bed sheets as togas. I roll my eyes at how basic their costumes are. I grab Maddy's hand. "Come on, let's go." I drag her to a different room, away from Zach's sight.

"Do you think he saw me?" Maddy has panic in her voice and she looks around.

I grab her arms to focus her. "Don't worry, I'm not going to let him touch you!"

Maddy nods as she calms down, unexpectedly pulling me into a hug. I panic for a little but hug her back. I've gotten more used to feeling her embrace, although the familiarity never diminishes the warmth and excitement it brings. The moment is ruined when we hear Zach's booming voice coming from the other room. "We should move somewhere else," Maddy yells close to my ear.

We decide to move towards the front of the house. If Zach just arrived that will be the last place he'll go. We stand around as a few other teens sit, talking on the stairs and smoking outside. I look towards Maddy, curiosity in my mind. What does she want to do? Will she hug me again? Will she pull me closer? Maddy meets my eyes and I feel a rush of electricity between us. I feel my heart beating and my body getting warm. We stare deeply into each other's eyes, and I begin having wishful thoughts again. I nervously begin inching myself closer to her, but she looks away.

"Umm, want some candy?" She points to the candy bowl that sits next to her door. We decide to play with the bowl for a while. Every time you reach for a piece of candy, the monster hand drops down on you. We try to see if we can grab a candy before the hand comes down on us. We're laughing and screaming each time it hits us, filling the air with joy.

As we're playing, out of the corner of my eye I notice the girl Sam was talking to stomping down the stairs with tears in her eyes. She brushes by us and heads outside. Maddy and I exchange looks and decided to head upstairs. Maddy has multiple rooms upstairs, not just spare bedrooms but offices, too. We can hear giggling and soft moans coming out from behind the closed doors.

Maddy rolls her eyes, knocking on a closed door. "As long as they're not in my room…"

I notice one of the room's doors cracked open and recognize the cardboard I had spent two days working on. "Sam?"

Maddy and I rush into the room to see Sam sitting there, blank faced. I get down to his level. "Sam, are you okay?"

Sam sighs, looking defeated.

"I'll give you guys some room to talk." Maddy begins to shut the door.

"But what about…?"

"I'll be fine, I'll stay right outside this door." She leaves and shuts the door. I'm nervous about Zach finding her, but my focus right now is on Sam.

"Sam, what happened?"

He lets out another long sigh. "I was talking to this girl. She invited me upstairs. She kissed me. I didn't like it so I pushed her off. Then she stormed out of the room." Sam says this all with a straight face. He doesn't seem upset about what happened, or surprised either. He acts like he knew this would happen.

I can't avoid the topic any longer. "Sam…are you gay?"

He hesitates for a bit, not sparing me a glance. "I don't know."

"Well, you said you don't find girls attractive." He doesn't say anything, just nods. "So, do you find boys attractive?"

Sam hesitates again, still not looking at me. "That's the thing. I've never felt attracted to boys either…just no one."

I take in the information. It could be that he just hasn't found anyone he likes yet, or it could be something else. I need more information, but luckily Sam decides to speak more, finally facing me he asks. "Do you think about kissing girls?"

I'm a little embarrassed about answering the question. "Yeah…"

"What about sex?"

"Uhh, that's a little personal…"

"Well, I've never thought about it." Sam goes back to looking at the ground. "I've never had dreams about kissing someone or having sex. Girls always show interest in me but I just don't feel anything towards them. I just…I don't understand."

I place my hand on his. "I understand." My voice is soft and comforting.

He looks up at me again, and this time I can see his eyes are red with tears starting to form. "You do?"

I begin recalling an old memory. "One time my dad sent me to a therapy group for people who identify as LGBTQ. Sort of a conversion thing…but I met a lot of other queer people there. One of them was this kid that said he was asexual and aromantic." Sam's eyebrow raises. "You know what it means?"

"Animals that are asexual are able to reproduce on their own."

"Yeah, okay, in science, but what this kid told me is that he doesn't feel sexual or romantic affection towards any gender. He doesn't feel it for anyone. He's asexual. And he's not the only one, it's a whole community." I wait to see his reaction. He's looking down and thinking. "You…you might be asexual."

I hear sniffling. I look over to Sam and see tears falling from his eyes. I start panicking at first but soon the sniffling turns to laughing, and Sam is sitting there smiling and crying.

"So I'm not alone." He throws his head back and laughs, his cheeks still damp from tears. "All this time, I thought there was something wrong with me, I thought that I wasn't normal, that I was born wrong, but I'm not alone." He begins crying more. "There's nothing wrong with me."

I can't help but cry for my friend. I remember this experience, when I learned what I was, and knew it was a normal thing. It feels like a huge weight being lifted from your shoulders. Watching Sam cry next to me, I can tell he's feeling the same thing. I lead his head to my shoulder and let him pour out the emotions.

It's about ten minutes before he gets all of his crying out. "Wow, I feel way better!" He stands up smiling, stretching his arms. "Everything just makes so much sense now!"

I get up with him. "When we get home you should look up more about asexuality, help you learn better."

Sam wipes his eyes and brings me into a hug. "I will," he softly whispers. He pulls away from me. "Don't you have a…'sexy' girl waiting for you?"

I roll my eyes. "Don't mock me now, not when we had such a moment."

He lightly laughs. "Sorry, I just feel like I have all this energy now! Like I can do anything."

I smile and pat his head. "Yes my dear son, you are free now."

He swats my hand away. "I'm not a kid."

"You sort of are. Finding out your sexuality is like being reborn."

He rolls his eyes. "Alright, now go and get your girlfriend." He pushes me towards the door.

"She's not my girlfriend."

"Not yet…"

I dismiss him with a flick of a hand, but when I leave the room, I can't help but have a cheesy grin. Maybe she might like me back? I look around the floor and don't see her.

Weird? Did she go to the bathroom or something? I notice from the corner of my eye one of the rooms cracked open; it was the room Maddy knocked on earlier. *Did she go into her room?*

I push open the door a bit more to see inside and my heart drops and the world goes dark. Maddy is on her bed with Zach, and they are passionately kissing. I thought for a second that Zach was forcing himself on Maddy, but when they stop, Maddy pulls his face close to hers again.

I don't notice I'm outside until I feel the cold air on my skin. I can barely see through the tears and everything is spinning. Through the spins I see an orange figure running towards me. They are trying to say something but I can't hear. I hear anything, just the sound of my heavy breathing. As I breathe more the figure grabs my shoulders. I can just make out "Michelle" being said but nothing else.

I feel my phone vibrating in my pocket. Picking it up, I see an unknown number calling. My body simply goes through the motions as I answer it.

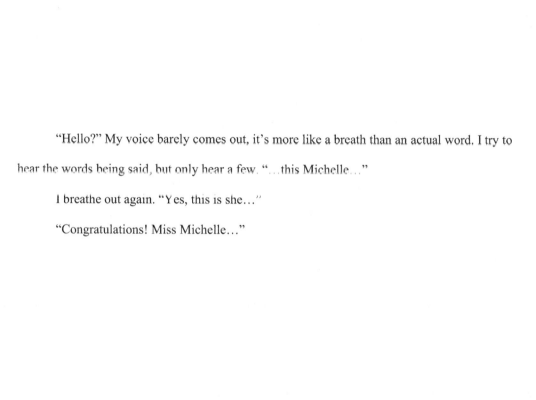

"Hello?" My voice barely comes out, it's more like a breath than an actual word. I try to hear the words being said, but only hear a few. "...this Michelle..."

I breathe out again. "Yes, this is she..."

"Congratulations! Miss Michelle..."

Chapter 18

"I can't believe she went back to him..." Chloe says as she watches Maddy sitting with Zach again.

Our once table of six has gone down to a table of five again. At the party, Zach had found Maddy by herself and wanted to talk to her. Maddy, being the goddess that she is, gave him a chance and apparently the talk ended with Zach on his knees begging for forgiveness. A few people witnessed it and it spread to the whole school, so them getting back together is the talk of town.

I can't even look at Maddy. Any time I hear her heels walking towards me, I look down or walk in a different direction. I know I shouldn't have been expecting anything from our relationship, I know that she's straight and I know what she needed was a friend, but I got my hopes up, and I ended up more heartbroken.

"This is all my fault..." Sam puts his head in his hands. "If you didn't come in to talk to me then..."

"Hey..." I rub Sam's back to comfort him. "I enjoyed our talk and if I knew what would happen. I would choose you again." Sam looks at me with his eyebrows raised. "Don't look surprised. You know how much I care about you." Everyone shifts in their chairs and exchanges glances with each other. I can tell everyone is worried about me with how silent they are. In class this morning I was waiting for Chloe to scream about her and Charlie, but she barely said anything, just a, "Yeah...we're official now..."

During art Sasha kept asking if I was okay every five seconds. She was the one who found me while I was having a mental breakdown. She said I looked as though I was choking on something, gasping for air and hunched over. She eventually found Sam, Charlie, and Chloe and the five of us left to bring me back to our house. I was catatonic for the rest of the weekend and apparently Zach tried entering my room a few times, but Sam and Charlie pushed him away.

Zach's been trying to rub it in my face any chance he gets. To avoid him I get breakfast early and end up taking the bus to school. Charlie volunteered to take the bus with me. I told him not to, but he came anyway.

I hate silence. I don't want my friends to pity me, I just want to go back to normal. "Guys, I'm okay, really. I never wanted a relationship with Maddy, I just..." I get quiet after realizing what I truly wanted. "I just wanted to save her."

Was I able to save her? I don't want to see her cry anymore, especially not over Zach, but maybe he learned his lesson and will change for good this time. She deserves better than him, but if he makes her happy, then do I have any right to stop that? I know Maddy and I've seen how much she's grown—she's smart enough to make her own choices now. I just have to hope I did enough for her.

My week is spent avoiding Zach and Maddy at all costs. Paul eventually notices something is up.

"Michelle, is there a reason you won't join us for dinner? If it's something I did..."

"No, Paul! You've been a great host and a great dad. Sam really appreciates what you've been doing."

He smiles and sits next to me on my bed. "I need to thank you for that. You made me realize that my boys are no longer my boys. They're their own people, and I can't control that."

"It's hard to let go."

"Yes, but back to you, if it's not me, is it one of the boys? Is it Zach?" I twitch when I hear his name. "So it is Zach... What did he do this time?"

"He won the girl, and now he wants to gloat."

"That boy was always a sore loser, cried whenever he didn't win, but when he did win, he would rub it into everyone's faces. I don't know what to do with that boy."

I give him a half smile. "Me neither."

"Well, I don't think it's fair for you to change your schedule for him. From now on we can do our own dinner up here. And in the morning I can drive you to school before I go to work."

I try to protest. "Paul you don't have to..."

He puts his hand up. "You've done a lot for this family in these few months. Especially for Sam and Charlie. It's the least I can do for you." My lip quivers and I fall into Paul's arms. I want to cry but I stop myself, hold it in. Paul holds me and all I can think is, *why couldn't I have had a father like this? It's not fair.* I squeeze him tighter as envy starts forming more and more in my chest. *It's not fair Zach gets a good father, it's not fair he gets to grow up in a nice house, it's not fair he gets everything. It's not fair. It's not fair. It's not fair.*

"Oww oww, you're squeezing me a little too tight!"

"Oh, I'm sorry." I pull away from Paul. "I didn't even realize."

He puts his hand up again. "You have a lot on your mind; how about I bring you some ice cream?"

I nod. "That would be very nice." Paul's right, I have a lot on my mind and I'm not being my usual self. I try not to be greedy. I feel I'm someone who should be grateful for what they do have instead of longing for something else, but I feel lately I've been wanting more. I've been having these dark thoughts filled with envy, a feeling I don't usually have, but lately it's consumed me. It's probably because I keep wanting things I know I can't have. Being at this house has given me a sense of false hope. I need to nip this in the bud before I can't return.

I want everything to go back to normal. I want to go back to normal. I walk into class and sit with Chloe.

"Hey, girlie!"

"Don't 'hey, girlie' me, I'm mad at you."

"Huh...but what did I..."

"After all the time and effort I spent on getting the two of you together, I get no thanks. The audacity." I shake my head.

"*What*! I..."

"Ms. McGhee, we just started class, can we save the outbursts for later?"

Chloe's face goes red and my mischievous grin returns.

"So, you were just teasing me..."

"Do you expect any less from me?" She rolls her eyes. "But in all seriousness, you haven't said anything about yours and Charlie's relationship. I've been following that shit like a weekly soap opera."

"I just didn't want to bring up any..."

I put my hand up. "Imma stop you right there. I never wanted a relationship with Maddy, okay? If she feels she'll be happy with shit-for-brains, then that's her choice."

Chloe pouts. "Okay."

"So, what happened?"

Chloe's cheerful self comes back and she recounts her love story.

"Okay, so the party just started and he went and grabbed us drinks and we were just talking with each other in the corner of the room and like, it was really intimate."

"Uh huh."

"So as we were getting a little more drunk and as the time was going by, Charlie was like 'I wanna talk to you about something,' and he was holding me and stuff, like I was practically sitting on him at that point."

"Okay…" At this point I'm struggling keeping up with Chloe. She is so hyper talking about this that her words start mashing together.

"He was like 'I really like you' and like, oh my god my heart was beating so fast like my knees were shaking, and so I told him, yeah I like you too…and then it was like awkward for a bit since we just both confessed to each other, but then we both started laughing about it and it was a cute moment and then, and *then*!"

She gets really excited for the next part. I have to shush her a bit so the teacher doesn't hear us.

"He was like, 'Can I kiss you?'"

My mouth springs open at this. I didn't think Charlie would be so bold.

"And so I was like, yeah…and then he leaned in and we kissed."

"Oh my god!" I feel happy for her. Since the first day I met her she has been pining for Charlie, and to think she's finally got him! *I'm envious…* I shake my head for a bit, trying to get rid of the bad thoughts that keep creeping up on me.

"Yeah, so we're official now."

I smile with her. "Finally!"

"I know!"

"Wait, so does this mean you're going to stop being my friend?"

"What? Why would I do that…"

"Oh you know…since you only befriended me to get close to him." I smile as her face blushes from embarrassment.

"That's *not* why!"

"Ms. McGhee, if you want to stand up and shout in a classroom you can join the theater club, but leave it out of math."

I hide my laughter as she sinks into her chair. "No fair teasing me like that."

"But I missed teasing you like this, you've all been weird around me lately and I just want things to go back to normal."

Chloe's eyes soften. "Okay, I understand…you can tease me a little, I guess."

"You're going to regret those words."

She puts her head on her desk in defeat. "I already do."

***

Our lunch table is back to being talkative again, especially with Chloe and Charlie being the new focus of the group.

"Charlie, you have no idea how much this girl stalked you."

"Sasha!"

"I mean, she knew your schedule, who you hung out with, what you did on the weekends…" Chloe shoots up and covers Sasha's mouth.

"Wow, I didn't know you liked me that much." Charlie winks at Chloe which makes her blush.

"I don't think I liked you that much…" Chloe twirls her hair in a flirtatious way.

Sasha and I both scream, "You did!"

"Well, to be fair, I was talking about you nonstop to Sam and Michelle."

"True, he would come into my room every night and cry over you." I do an overexaggerated sad voice, "What if Chloe rejects me? What if it ruins our friendship!" Charlie throws fries at me. "Oww!" I wipe the fry juice from my face. "So, now that you and Chloe are official, are you going to invite her to your band rehearsal?"

Hearing this makes Chloe's eyes light up. She turns to face him with stars in her eyes, alongside a healthy dose of pleading.

Charlie looks down for a bit, his eyes somewhere else, looking at something painful. He eventually looks at Chloe. "Yeah, you can come." Chloe cheers as Charlie looks towards me. "You should come, too."

"Me?" I'm taken aback for a bit. It makes sense he would take Chloe, but I'm surprised he wants me to go.

Charlie smiles. "Yeah, you." The way he smiles tells me he's ready to let me in and tell me everything. I feel relieved I'll finally be able to know all of Charlie.

"So what day…"

BUM BUM BUM. The whole lunchroom turns to see five members of the marching band coming in playing some music, followed by a guy from the football team rolling out a red carpet. The carpet leads to Maddy's table. The same football player stands Maddy up and leads her to the center of the carpet, and also right in front of everyone in the lunchroom. I notice how she looks around, embarrassed by this.

What I see next causes a pain in my heart. Zach walks down the carpet holding a bouquet of flowers the size of his face. He smiles and hands them to Maddy, whose face is red with embarrassment. I can see her mouth, "What are you doing?" Zach gets down on one knee and I think I'm going to vomit. The whole school starts to cheer.

"Come on, let's get out of here." I feel Sam pull on my arm. "You don't have to see this."

I nudge him off. "No. I want to." I turn and see the concerned faces of my friends. "Guys, like I said, if Maddy is happy then I'm okay with it." I take a deep breath and continue watching the sight unfold in front of my eyes.

"Maddy, you're my girl, you've always been my girl. You're the only one for me." I roll my eyes hearing this. *Yeah, except for the times you dumped her for other girls.* "I know I made some mistakes in the past…" *Some mistakes?* "But you never know how much you love something 'til you let it go, and after losing you, I realized how much I love you… Maddy, will you go to homecoming with me?"

"Ugh, so it was a stupid homecoming proposal? I forgot that's coming up." Sasha turns around to stop watching the proposal.

"Yeah, it's so lame!" Chloe turns away, too.

"When I ask you to homecoming, I want to make it more private and personal."

Chloe's eyes light up again "When!"

Zach's football friends bring out a large sign that says, "Will you go to homecoming with me?" written on it. Maddy looks shocked, but also, uncomfortable. As the kids in the lunchroom cheer, she darts her eyes away and steps back.

"I…I…" Maddy is hesitating and her body is shaking. Zach waits there on his knee, with a big smile on his face, for her response. I know why he's doing a grand gesture. He wants to show off to me. He wants me to know that Maddy is his property and that I can never have her, that she will always go back to him.

"No."

At the sound of the word the cheering changes to a collection of "What?" and "Huh?" Zach's smile begins to fade.

"You're…you're saying no to me?"

Maddy's eyes are deeply focused. "I'm saying no. I don't want to go to homecoming with you."

The crowd begins to "oooooh" as Zach's smile disappears for a moment, but then he tries to laugh it off. "Baby…you can't be serious, right?"

Maddy's demeanor is unchanging. She doesn't flinch, she's just direct and forward. "I am being serious… And I want to break up."

A mixture of shocked reactions arise from the crowd. Zach's stunned face turns to anger. "Break up?"

"I'm breaking up with you."

Zach gets up at this point. "Baby I…I promised I'd change! I'm never going to hurt you ever again! I swear I…" He clings to her.

She pushes him back. "Don't start, I don't want to hear the pet names and that's not the problem." Maddy's eyes grow soft and there is a subtle downturn of the corners of her mouth. "I just don't like you anymore."

He takes a step back. "Don't like me…"

"Yeah, I just don't like you… I don't have fun on our dates, I don't like kissing you and…I bet you don't even know what my favorite color is!"

"I…I know what your favorite color is! It's pink!"

No, it's pale blue…

Maddy shakes her head in disappointment and backs away. "Zach, it's over, for good this time, okay? I'm done with you, forever." Maddy turns and starts walking away.

"Maddy! You can't dump me!" Zach is calling after her but she keeps walking…towards me.

As she approaches me. I look around to see if there is someone or something else she is heading towards, but no, she is coming to me.

She grabs my hand and with a warm smile on her face says, "Let's go."

I don't say anything. I am too stunned to speak. Is this real? Am I just dreaming? She leads me out of the lunchroom, just like on the night of the bonfire, but this time, she's holding my hand. She intertwines her fingers with mine and pulls me faster. We are soon running down the halls together, laughing, enjoying the freedom we both have. We run, hand in hand, to her car and instinctively get into it.

Maddy drives away as we catch our breath and laugh together. "That felt good!"

"Dang, Vitis, never saw that coming from you."

"I feel so free now! Like I can go anywhere!" She looks at the road filled with determination.

"Yeah, where are we going?"

Her smile fades. "Oh, I didn't actually think of that. I just knew I wanted to get away."

An idea pops in my head. "I know somewhere we can go. It might take a while, is that okay?"

She smiles; the further the better.

***

On our ride Maddy tells me the whole story.

"After you went in the room to talk to Sam, I sat next to the door waiting, but then Zach got there. I shot up, frightened of what he might do.

"He said, 'Wait, wait, Maddy, I just want to talk I promise, just give me a few seconds.'

"I obviously didn't want to give him any seconds, but I guess I was still under his spell a little bit. We spent too long together and had such a history, I just couldn't say no. We went to my room to talk but left the door open just in case, and that's when he got down on his knees sobbing, 'Maddy! Please! I was wrong! I didn't see it before but now I see how wrong I've treated you! How much I must have hurt you! Please, Maddy, don't leave me. I need you! I am nothing without you!'

"It was everything I wanted to hear from him. I wanted to hear him admit that he was wrong, I wanted him to say I was the only one for him, and I finally got it, so I caved. It was so stupid, I'm sorry, Michelle." Maddy's lips curl down and her body slumps.

I rub her back to reassure her. "It's not easy to get over a four-year relationship, not that I would know, but I don't think you're stupid."

She looks at me with sorrowful eyes. "But I hurt you."

"Well, yeah, you sort of did." Sorry, Maddy, I am an honest person. "But I just wanted you to be happy, and if Zach had truly changed and would make you happy, then I was fine with that."

"It did seem like he had changed, but during the last week, as he was taking me on dates and treating me right, I realized that...I wasn't having fun."

"Dates were boring?"

"Not just that, our conversations were boring. He would talk about football and only ask me about cheerleading. He asked if I was still going to Ohio State and he even said bad things about you."

I sigh. "Well, to be fair, I was also saying bad things about him to you so I guess we're equal."

"Yeah, but unlike you, I didn't agree with what he was saying."

I don't want to ask what was said because I don't want to know. I assume it has something to do with my sexuality or something and I just don't care enough about Zach's opinion.

"So you decided to end it?"

"Yeah. I also realized that I just wasn't attracted to him anymore, and thinking back at it, when was the last time he made my heart race or we had a deep and meaningful conversation? I don't think the latter ever happened, and I think the last time my heart skipped a beat was four years ago. Thinking about it now, why did I hold on to him for so long?"

"Probably because of the emotional abuse. By dumping you and asking you out again, it made you want to fight for him, even if you stopped liking him."

Maddy pouts. "Ugh, I can't believe I wasted my high school life on him."

"Hey, you still got the rest of your senior year, he didn't ruin all of your high school life." I try to cheer Maddy up, but she is still distressed about everything. So I try a different approach. "I wasted my high school life with no friends."

"You didn't have a lot of friends at your school?"

"No, I had no friends." I see the way Maddy's eyes get wide and then soften. "I would spend lunch in the art room so I wouldn't have to be near other people, I would always ask to work alone for group projects, and I just got used to not having friends. I was ready for Chloe and Sasha to ditch me after the first day here but they stuck around... I thought the boys would find me gross, but they've stayed with me, it's weird."

"So I guess that makes you like me." I'm surprised by Maddy's comment and wait to see what she means. "You and I both got comfortable with a bad situation so we never tried to change it."

I laugh as I begin to understand. "Well, would you look at that, maybe we are meant for each other." I try to sound like one of those fortune tellers and Maddy laughs.

"See, you're always able to make me laugh. With Zach, I would just fake laugh with him. He didn't get my sense of humor at all...actually, I don't think he knew me at all. I just realized he probably only liked me for my looks."

"Damn, if he only saw you for your looks then he's missing out."

She rolls her eyes. "Oh please..."

I chuckle. "What? I'm being serious." I give her a smirk.

"Uh huh..."

We joke around for the rest of the car ride, moving on from our conversation of Zach to anything else. I get to tell her about Chloe and Charlie.

"Oh my god, finally! We were all waiting for that to happen!"

"Yeah, and Charlie invited us to see his band practice."

"Really? Wow, it's been so long since I've heard him play."

"He used to perform a lot?"

"Yeah at parties and such, but one day he stopped."

"Do you know why?"

Maddy shrugs. "Nope, and Zach never said anything. He never talked about his brothers."

"Why am I not surprised?"

After an almost three-hour long car ride, we make it to Dayton, Ohio.

"Dayton? I haven't been here in years." Maddy looks around the tall buildings as she follows my directions.

"I've never been here, but it's still smaller than Philly."

She rolls her eyes. "If you've never been here, then why did you want to come here."

"To show you something. Pull in here."

She pulls into a spot across from a large white building. "What is thi—"

"Come on." I interrupt her and grab her hand, pulling her inside.

As we enter, she is frozen in place. "Stay here for a moment." I go talk to the front desk, while Maddy gets to stand and take in the sights of the museum.

It isn't a large art museum, at least not like the ones I've been to in major cities, but the museum's interior exudes an air of sophistication, with high ceilings adorned by ornate chandeliers. Sunlight streams through grand windows, illuminating carefully curated exhibits. Hushed whispers echo, blending with the subtle sounds of footsteps on polished marble floors. Priceless artworks adorn the walls, each piece telling a silent story.

"Alright, this way." I grab Maddy's hand and lead her though the museum.

"So, you wanted to come to a museum…" As she passes by various paintings she comes to the realization. "Is this *the* museum?" Excitement starts rising in her voice. "Did you…!"

"Shhh." I have to turn around and shush her before she disturbs the other guests. I lead her into a restricted area for staff only. The large closet is filled with different kinds of paintings, canvases leaned against one another, some boldly expressing abstract visions, while others capture serene landscapes or intimate portraits. I search each of them, looking for a familiar one and I find it.

"Okay, come over here." I lead her in front of a painting and her eyes widen in awe. A mixture of surprise and joy plays across her features and an involuntary smile tug at the corners of her lips. She studies the painting as tears fill her eyes and she covers her mouth to control the overwhelming emotion.

I like to paint beautiful things, and the most beautiful thing in Ohio is Maddy.

Chapter 19

The painting is a sort of portrait of Maddy. I painted her,. shoulders up, and since her hair hangs down her body, I painted it into waves that cover the bottom on the canvas. The rest of her hair is adorned with seashells and starfish. I wanted to capture the mermaid essence she gives off. I made her face glittering and shining, just like the night of the bonfire. I wanted her face to resemble an angel.

Maddy uncovers her mouth and tries to speak. "This is…"

"The most beautiful thing I've seen since coming to Ohio."

Maddy has tears running down her face and it becomes hard for her to talk. "It's…it's amazing."

"I got the call on the night of the Halloween party. I could barely hear them but my painting was selected. I was a little too emotional that night to celebrate… I still haven't told the others yet. When we got here I told the security guard I wanted to make sure my piece was alright and he told me where to go."

She stands there admiring the work. "I just can't believe you painted me!"

I chuckled to myself a bit. "I told you when we first met." I look her in the eyes with a smile. "You're beautiful."

I don't notice Maddy's blushing face since I go back to checking on my painting. I realize that I haven't heard from Maddy but when I turn to her, her face is a soft pink, her eyes soft and focused, and her eyebrows raised in surprise.

Before I can say anything, I feel her lips press against mine. The gay panic returns and I just stand there, not moving, my eyes widening every second. She pull back from me, a twinkle in her eyes.

She looks away. "Sorry…I just…" I'm not going to let her apologize. I pull her in for another kiss. She's stunned for a moment but begins kissing me back. I don't care if I'm being greedy anymore, I'll let myself give in if it means I can share this kiss. As we kiss, I feel all my envious feelings melt away, all of the pent of anger I had washes away like waves returning to the ocean. The memories of Paul being a good father, of Chloe and Charlie with their relationship, and of Zach kissing Maddy, all of the jealous rage caused from those moments seems to vanish, filled instead with the warmth of Maddy's lips.

It seems all I needed was Maddy. I've been denying it to myself, saying I just wanted her to be happy, but that was all a lie. I want to be with Maddy. If I could have anything it would be Maddy. I'm not satisfied with just being on the side, I want to be next to her. These feelings of want and need flood in more and more as I sink into Maddy's kiss. Everything I've ever wanted in life, everything I wish I had, I feel like I've finally achieved it.

We let go for air, both trying to catch our breath as we look each other in the eyes. Our faces share the same pink hue and I feel our heart beats are in sync. In that moment, a profound connection seems to envelop us, as if our hearts are composing a silent symphony.

We are both in shock, not sure what to do next. I clear my throat. "So I take it you like the painting?"

Maddy breaths out a laugh. "Ha, of course that would be the first thing you say." She takes a deep breath and sighs. "Yes. I like the painting." We laugh at how effortlessly joy can weave its way into the simplest moments, creating memories that linger like the warmth of sunshine.

"We should probably leave the closet now," Maddy whispers, trying to be seductive.

I know she's trying to be cool but she set it up so perfectly I have to respond. "So you're ready to come out of the closet?"

As her face contorts, trying to figure out what I said, I begin to giggle, and as her face turns red, realizing what I said, I start to laugh uncontrollably.

She playfully hits my arm. "You…" But I just keep laughing. Her eyes narrow and her tone drops. "That was the worst joke ever."

"Nah. It was brilliant."

Maddy starts laughing at this point. "Terrible joke." I just stand there, laughing even more. "Ugh, let's go." She grabs my hand and drags me back into the museum lobby. We attract some attention from the small crowd but I don't care. I eventually run ahead of her and get to the car first, laughing more freely now.

She catches up to me. "Jerk."

I smile. "Yeah, but isn't that why you like me?"

She smiles back. "Yeah, probably."

We slip back into the car. "So you're admitting that you like me?"

"Was me kissing you not enough?"

"I don't know, I kissed a boy once and uh, yeah, I didn't like him."

Maddy giggles. Okay well, do you like me?"

I laugh. "Ha, you had me at 'stay away from my man, bitch.'"

Her mouth falls open. "I did not say it like that!"

I tilt my head back and forth. "Ehh, you basically did."

"I did not!"

The rest of the drive home involves me telling her about my feelings for her and her sharing how she came to realize she liked me.

"I think I enjoyed our conversations and our time together. I felt like I could talk to you about anything and not feel embarrassed or judged. And after Zach and I got back together..." I frown at the mention of his name. "I realized that, while with him, I kept thinking of you."

A rose hue appears on my cheeks and a shy smile reveals my feelings of embarrassment and flattery. "What's with you?" I get even quieter. "Why are you saying such embarrassing stuff?"

"Whoa, are you getting embarrassed now?"

I comically sink into my chair. "Maybe."

"Even after calling me sexy on Halloween?"

She's trying to mess with me again but I'm not going to let her win. With a smug smile I add, "Was I wrong?"

Her face goes red and she hangs her head in defeat. "Why are you like this?"

"You can't out-cheek the queen of cheeky."

She rolls her eyes and mumbles under her breath, "Queen of cheeky."

"Don't act like you don't like it."

She smiles. "You make things fun, I guess."

The three-hour long car ride goes by in a flash, as we share stories, laughter, and the scenic beauty outside the window, turning a long drive to a delightful time.

By the time we get back to the house it's already dark out, and there are no other cars on the road. We pull up to the driveway and I stop her. "Just let me out here."

"Why, it's a long walk. Just let me drive you…"

"No, what if Zach is waiting at the top? I don't want you to have to confront him."

Her eyebrows raise in concern. "Shit, I almost forgot, are you going to be okay?"

I pop open the car door. "Yeah of course, I have Sam and Charlie there. They'll protect me."

As I try to leave, she grabs my wrist. "Zach is strong."

"But I trust Sam and Charlie, they won't let anything happen to me," I reassure her and she drops my wrist. I begin the walk up the driveway, not sure what will be waiting for me at the top.

Each of my steps get heavier and heavier, a silent acknowledgment of the impending doom that awaits me at the end of the path. As I see the house lights come into view, the steps become harder and I start to shake. He's the first thing I notice. Zach is sitting on the footsteps of the house. He looks like a statue, frozen in a sitting position. Due to the light, I can't see his face, but he's resting his chin on his hands in a stern way, not looking relaxed at all. I try to slow down my steps but he notices me.

He charges at me with his hand above his head, ready to slam down on me. "You little bitch!" I can't even respond so I just brace myself but the punch never comes. I open my eyes to see Charlie standing in front of me, his hand out protecting me. Sam is holding onto Zach's arms to hold him back.

"Let go of me, this bitch is going to die tonight!" Zach pushes hard on Sam, but Sam holds on, the years of carving wood giving him enough muscle to hold his own against Zach.

"Are you okay?" Charlie whispers to me.

"Yeah, I'm okay, I knew you guys would be here."

Charlie smiles. "When we got home Zach refused to go inside. He insisted on staying outside and waiting for you. Sam and I tried pushing him in but he wouldn't budge, so we waited outside, too."

"You guys have just been waiting out here the whole time?" I knew the boys cared about me but I didn't think they would stand for hours in the cold just so I wouldn't get hurt. A smile grows on me, even in this terrifying situation.

"We aren't going to let him hurt you." He grabs my hand and we slowly walk around. "Come on." We tiptoed by, Charlie's body always facing Zach, becoming a human shield for me.

Zach notices we're trying to escape and tries to lunge at me again. "Stupid bitch! I don't know what you told Maddy, but you're going to pay for it!"

My jaw clenches. "What did I say to Maddy?" I'm in disbelief of his idiocy. "I didn't do shit, she just figured out how much of an asshole you are!"

"*What did you say?*" Zach pushes harder against Sam and I see Sam struggling. I know I shouldn't have engaged in an argument with him, especially with Sam barely holding him back, but I'm not going to let him shift the blame onto someone else.

"You made Maddy miserable and you couldn't even tell! You cheated on her all the time and made her feel paranoid of everyone around her!"

"What? I made her paranoid?" He stops pushing on Sam for a brief moment. "She was a bitch to everyone in school! How was that my fault?"

I feel the anger in me rising up. Is he really this stupid or just toying with me? I don't know or care, I'm not going to let him say these things about Maddy. I let my anger get the best of me. "She was mean to other girls *because of you*! She was so afraid of you cheating on her, she wanted to scare off all of the girls! You made her do it, *it was all you*!"

He starts to lunge at me again, the veins in his forehead practically popping out. "I *never* told her to bully anyone!"

"You made her feel *crazy*! She thought she had no other choice! Why can't your dumb ass understand that?"

Zach's shaking stops, but his glare does not. Now he's actually angry. He turns to face Sam and knees him in the stomach. Sam falls to the ground.

Charlie push me towards the house. "Go inside! Run!"

Before I can say anything, Charlie rushes up to Zach but he punches him in the face, also knocking Charlie down.

I run as fast as I can to the door. As I get to it, with Zach on my tail, Paul opens up. "What the *hell* is going on out here?"

It's the first time I've ever seen Paul angry. His usual upbeat and positive personality is replaced by a storm of fury, transforming his smiling face into a tempest of wrath. Both Zach and I stop and from Zach's reaction I can tell he also hasn't seen Paul this angry.

Charlie gets up, holding his face, and Sam waddles over holding his stomach. Ashamed of how they are acting, the two of them avert their eye contact from Paul.

"Is *anyone* going to answer me?" Paul's booming voice sends shivers down my spine and I find myself more afraid of him at the moment than of Zach.

Zach, with a small shaking voice, tries to answer. "I, uh…"

"He's trying to kill Michelle!" Charlie shouts from below. He's made his way up to the steps with me. "He's mad at her because his girlfriend dumped him."

Zach's anger turns to Charlie now, but Charlie, with his face already swelling from the hit, stands his ground.

Paul looks at Zach, a mixture of disgust and disappointment over his face. "Why the hell are you mad at Michelle if your girlfriend dumped you?"

Surprisingly, Zach tries to confidently defend his actions. "She stole my Maddy away! She fed her lies about me!"

"The fact that you're calling her 'my Maddy' just shows why she dumped you! You only ever saw her as an option, something to possess rather than a human!" Even with Paul yelling at us, I still don't want Zach saying anything about Maddy. Even hearing her name come out of his mouth makes my blood boil.

Zach tries to defend himself again. "You don't know how I feel!"

But Paul puts his hand up, shutting Zach up in a moment. Paul addresses Zach, his voice lower but with a stern rage still in it. "I don't want to hear anything about Michelle doing this or that to you. You *NEVER*,"—when he screamed the word never all four of us jumped—"never hit a woman. I thought I had taught you better."

Slowly Paul's rage turns to disappointment. Zach tries a "But…"

But once again Paul shuts him up. "I don't want to hear it! It's your own damn fault you lost your girlfriend! If you can't keep her, you can't keep her! Don't blame Michelle for your shortcomings." After that, Zach has nothing to say. "Come on Michelle."

Paul escorts me into the house, Sam and Charlie following afterwards. But Zach stays outside for a little longer.

Paul makes sure I get all the way to my room before letting me go. "Michelle, I'm so sorry for that boy. I don't know what's wrong with him." Paul looks down with a frown, seeming not only disappointed in Zach, but also disappointed in himself. "I don't want you to feel afraid to come to the house because Zach is here. You should feel safe." The sadness in Paul's voice makes my heart hurt. He is too nice of a man to be this sad over me.

"Paul, I'm not afraid…" I reassure him. "With you, Sam, and Charlie here, I never feel afraid." Sam and Charlie are also in my room, standing up better now, but Charlie's face is red from the hit.

Paul gets up and hugs his two boys. "I'm proud of you two. Keep protecting her, okay?" The boys are stiff and only lightly pat their dad's back; they probably aren't used to getting hugs from him. "And Charlie…" Charlie looks to his dad, awaiting his words. "Go get an ice pack." Paul smiles and pats Charlie's shoulder, saying goodnight as he leaves us alone in my room. We all breathe.

"You really should get an ice pack."

"I will…I just wanted to make sure you're okay,"

I give a soft smile. "I'm fine, I always knew I would be. I knew you guys would be there. You guys are like my older brothers."

They exchange looks with each other and smile. "You're our sister now, we gotta watch out for you." Sam says, squeezing my hand for reassurance.

"But are you guys older? I could be older…"

We looked at each other for a bit, but Sam speaks first. "July 31st."

"Damn! I'm August 13th."

Charlie pats my head. "Go get some sleep, little sis, we'll talk to you in the morning."

I push him away. "Eww, don't treat me like a baby."

"Want me to tuck you in?" Sam motions at the covers.

"No! Go away!" I throw my pillows at the boys and they playfully laugh as they leave. "And Charlie, get an ice pack!"

Somehow we survived the night. I don't know what it'll be like moving forward, but with Sam and Charlie here, I feel I have nothing to worry about.

Chapter 20

I take a deep breath and look for my confidence, the hand squeezing mine helping me get it. Maddy and I open the doors and walk into the lunchroom, hand in hand, and no cares in the world.

Walking to our table makes me feel like we're on a runway. Everyone sitting turns their heads to face us. We can hear gasps coming from the crowd, but I don't care. I have Maddy next to me, and with her there, I feel invincible.

"Hi, guys, I'm back." Maddy shyly says as she finds her seat at our table.

Everyone exchanges looks with each other for a bit, but eventually relaxes and smiles.

Sasha smirks. "Yeah, I guess we missed you." She tries to make it sound nonchalant, but you can feel the affection in her.

Chloe jumps to her. "Girlie, we were so worried when you went back to that asshole, Michi over here was all 'if she's happy, then I'm happy,' but I'm like, no. No way she would be happy with that man. And I'm glad you saw that."

Maddy thinks Chloe's impersonation of me is funny, I do not. "Well, if it wasn't for Michelle, I probably wouldn't have been able to see how terrible he was to me. I guess I thought that that's what love was."

"But it's not!" Chloe shoots up, energy fueling her as she declares her opinions. "Now that I'm in a relationship, I know what a good relationship is supposed to look like. And Charlie cares about me, but he's also a good guy to everyone."

Charlie rubs his eye. "Babe, stop, you're embarrassing me!"

"What! I'm being honest! Like the other night we were talking on the phone…" Chloe starts addressing the whole table, talking like she's about to break the biggest news story.

"Wait, babe…"

"And he told me he couldn't sleep unless he could listen to my voice!"

"Chloe, babe, that's…enough!" Charlie is playfully putting his hand over Chloe's mouth to quiet her, but you can tell from his panicked expression he really does want to hush her.

The rest of us frown at him. "Dude, that's super cringe, even for me."

"Michelle, you've said way worse things."

"True, but at least I wasn't cringy."

Maddy snickers. "Please…"

"I…" I try to come up with a defense but I have nothing. "Okay yeah, so I also am the worst. I get it."

Maddy puts her hand on mine. "Yeah, but that's why I like you." Her smile beams down on me. I had almost forgotten the goddess that she is.

"Ugh, so now we're the couples table?" We all look towards Sasha who is uninterested. "Everyone here is in a relationship with each other?"

"Well, Sash, there is one other person in our group." Chloe nods her head in the direction of Sam, who looks up in confusion. He clearly wasn't paying attention, instead looking down at his phone the whole time.

"What?"

"I'm saying you and Sasha are the only single people at this table. Maybe you could get together."

"Yeah I'll pass…" Sasha says, without skipping a beat.

Chloe tries pleading with her. "But what if…"

"I have someone I like already." Chloe is about to open her mouth but Sasha puts up her hand. "I will tell you when I'm ready."

"Okay then, but what about Sam? Do you have someone you like?"

I have to seal my lips as Sam looks at me for help. I want to say something but it's up to Sam. He must see how uncomfortable I look so he speaks up.

"Actually… after talking with Michelle and doing my own research, I've discovered that I'm asexual."

There's silence. I give him a reassuring thumbs-up to make him feel better, but he's still looking to the group for responses.

"Asexual like the animals that are able to reproduce on their own?" Sasha's the first to ask, confused but not trying to be harmful

Sam lets out a slight chuckle. "No, well, sort of. It means that I don't feel sexual attraction to any gender. So, I like people as friends, but when it comes to a romantic partner or sexual partner, I don't feel anything. So yeah." Sam smiles, looking at the group.

There is a collective "ooh" from the group as people start to understand.

"So that's why you rejected all of those girls." Chloe says, rubbing her chin like a detective.

"Yeah, at first I thought that maybe I just hadn't found the right person yet, but after what Michelle told me, and after looking into it more, I'm like, yeah that's me. I'm asexual." I feel proud seeing how open Sam is being with his sexuality. I mouth, "Mommy's proud," and he rolls his eyes.

The group nods and a collection of "nice" and "that's cool" are heard.

I reach my hand out to Sam. "Welcome to the club, my friend."

"What club?"

I place my other hand onto Maddy's. "The queer club."

"Me too!" We all pause to look at the unfamiliar voice. A boy I've never seen before stands at our table.

"Patrick Winston?"

"You know him, Charlie?" I ask

"Yeah, we have science together..."

"Umm..." Patrick sits down at our table. "The truth is, I've known I was gay for a while, but obviously I couldn't say anything. I didn't want to be bullied or harassed...but seeing how brave you two have been"—he motions to Maddy and I—"I want to be brave."

No one responds at first, but I take a liking to the guy. I pat the table. "Come have a seat, my dude."

He nods and sits with us, smiling like a kid opening presents on Christmas.

"Hi, did I hear you're also gay?" Another unknown boy appears next to Patrick, sitting down without even asking. "I always thought I was the only one at our school!"

Patrick gets excited. "Yeah, me too!" The two start talking and sharing experiences, the rest of us sitting there silently, looking at each other for answers.

Sasha leans over to me and whispers, "Dude, I think you guys started some gay revolt."

I snort. "Gay revolt?"

"Yeah, people are now more comfortable being open about their sexuality. I think you started it."

I shrug. "Well, wasn't my attention, but I support the gays."

I sort of became a trendsetter around school. People come up to me and talk to me about their sexuality and feelings. People open up about how they are confused about how they feel but my bravery is helping them understand. I don't like attention so the whole situation makes me very uncomfortable, but I'm not going to turn away a fellow queer.

While there are a lot of people who support me or people who don't care, there are a few who still give me disgusted stares, especially those on the football and cheerleading teams. They won't approach me due to Sam and Charlie threatening to beat them up, but that doesn't stop the staring and whispering.

"Dude, you're like the gay Buddha." Sasha and I are in art club talking about everything.

"How am I the gay Buddha?"

"You're teaching people the gay way.

"That's not a thing and I'm pretty sure that's not what Buddha did."

"Yeah, whatever." She continues putting the finishing touches to a hyper-realistic painting of a dog, a commission she got a while ago. "I'm still mad at you, though."

"For not telling you about my art piece getting picked?"

She puts down her paintbrush and whips her phone in my face, her eyebrows pointed down at me to show her anger. "'Oh BTW, my piece got selected for the art exhibit, sorry forgot to tell you, lolz.'" She reads out my text with an annoyed expression.

"I had a lot going on." I know I have no excuse for not telling them sooner. Everyone was pretty pissed off that I sent a text telling them. Maddy ended up being the only person who I told in person. They understood why I didn't tell them right away but I guess they're still upset.

"I was wondering what that phone call was. To think it was the news, and you didn't have the best reaction?"

I rub my temple. I don't want to think about that night. "Yeah, I didn't even understand what they were saying. I called back the next day once I was feeling better just to confirm."

"Well, despite getting the news late, I'm proud of you." Sasha struggles saying proud. I've noticed she isn't one to give many compliments.

"I'm also very proud of you, Michelle." Ms. Park stands next to me, emotionless as usual. I don't know if she's being sincere, though—her voice has no softness to it, it's just direct, like she's making a business deal or something. "I'll make sure to be at the showing." With that monotone response, she walks off.

"Wow, I've never seen Ms. Park that happy before." Sasha is genuinely impressed.

"What? You're joking, right?"

"No, usually she's all…" Sasha does a face that resembles a zombie. "But today she was all…" Sasha does a blank face with the corners of her mouth slightly turned upwards.

"How can you tell? I can never tell what she's thinking! Does she even like me?"

"I've had Ms. Park for four years. She's quiet and keeps to herself a lot, but she cares about her students. You see the mountain of papers on her desk?" She nods her head towards the desk.

"Yeah…"

"Those are students' artwork. She's going through them and making the best art portfolios for them, and then she's helping them find the best art schools. She takes a while because she knows what art schools are looking for and wants to make sure the portfolio is perfect. My paintings are somewhere in there. She also recommended me schools that would suit my talent and my career in life."

"Huh, guess that explains why she asked about college the first day I met her."

"Yeah, she really cares about us, even if it doesn't seem like it. She's doing her best to make us succeed."

Looking at Ms. Park working behind her desk, I begin to see her in a new light. Instead of a teacher too busy working to focus on her students, she's too busy focusing on her students to work. I begin to wonder if she went and found that competition specifically for me.

There are clearly a lot of things I don't know about the people of this town yet. A lot more queer people, friendly people, kind people. But I still have about eight months left here—plenty more time to learn about people.

"Alright, see you, Michi." Sasha and I part and I skip to the car. Although today I'm not going home with Sam, I'm meeting Chloe, Maddy, and Charlie, and we are going to watch Charlie practice!

Sam's waiting by the car, but probably just so I won't have to wait alone. Zach is banned from riding in the car, so instead he's getting rides from his friends on the football team.

"Hey." Sam smiles.

"Hey, happy you came out to your friends?"

"Yeah, it felt nice…but I'm not happy with you." His smile melts into a pout.

I sigh. "About not telling you about the exhibit?"

He affirmed, "About not telling you about the exhibit."

"Sorry, I wanted to tell you sooner but…"

"I know…and I forgive you, but I was still mad."

I look down, disappointed in myself for making him upset.

"Which is why I held off on telling you my big news."

I look up at him with excitement. I can tell by his eye avoidance what he's going to say, and a large grin slowly appears on my face.

"I ended up getting an order on my website."

I jump up from the joy inside me. "Really?! What did they order? How much? Give me all the details!" At this point I'm jumping up and down, like a toddler waiting to get candy.

He smiles and tries to calm me down. "Okay, I'm going to tell you!" I stop bouncing to focus on Sam. "I actually got a large order from a small cafe opening in Dayton. They wanna use my work for their furniture. 3...2...1..."

I explode in a scream. "Oh my *god*! That's *huge*!"

Sam covers his ears. "I know, I know."

But my excitement doesn't stop. "A whole store? In a major city? Think about how many people are going to see your stuff!"

"Yeah, I know. It's going to take me a bit of time, but they paid me half up front so I can use it to buy supplies, and I talked the school into letting me come work on weekends."

I can't contain my joy. I jump up and wrap my arms around Sam's neck, tears starting to form in my eyes. "I'm so happy for you!"

"Umm, excuse me, what's going on here?" Maddy steps between us, pushing me away from Sam. I giggle to myself seeing how jealous Maddy is getting.

"Maddy, be careful, babe, you're dealing with a celebrity here." Maddy looks at Sam, confused.

He flushes from embarrassment. "I'm not going to be a celebrity..."

I ignore him and keep bragging to Maddy. "Sam's wood work is going to be used as furniture for a big cafe in a major city!"

"It's a rather small place and I wouldn't consider Dayton a major city."

Maddy ignores him as she gasps, "Wow, should we get his autograph now?"

"You know, babe, my room is already filled with Sam Owens originals, people are going to be so jealous."

Maddy plays along with me as Sam gets more embarrassed. "Wow, a Sam Owens original! Those could go for a fortune soon."

Sam hangs his head in defeat. "Please stop."

Maddy and I laugh playfully with him. "But I'm all seriousness, this is a huge deal! Have you told Paul?"

"Yeah, I told him last night. He gave me a hug and told me he's glad I found my calling." As I see Sam's warm smile, all I can think is *Paul is really a good father.* But this time I don't feel envious, just proud of my friend.

As I feel Maddy's arm brushing up next to mine, I remember something. "By the way, Maddy, how was cheer practice?"

Her body drops and she takes a long sigh. "Some of the girls tried to have me kicked off, the others voted to have me step down as captain. Eventually my coach said if anyone could do more back handsprings than me they would be the new captain."

"And?"

"And I'm still the cheer captain." Maddy has a smug smile as she flips her hair. *That's my girl.*

"Yo." Charlie finally pulls up with Chloe at his side. "My friend is almost here to pick us up, we should get ready."

"Oh my god, Charlie! Sam just…" I want to explode about Sam's achievement, to scream it to the world, but I stop myself, knowing that it's something Sam has to share, not me. I look at Sam, worried he'll be upset, but Sam looks calm, a soft smile across his face.

"I got an order to make furniture for a cafe in Dayton."

"Holy shit, dude, that's awesome."

"Well, Michelle inspired me to make a website and put my work out there."

"Does that mean I get a share of the profit?"

"Don't ruin this moment." Although he says that, Sam and I laugh over the moment. "If there's nothing else, I'm going to head out now. I have things to do."

He heads towards the driver's side door. "Wait!" I run towards him. "One last hug." I pull him close to me and whisper, "I'm so proud of you."

He holds me back. "Thank you."

I can feel Maddy glaring at us so I let go and rush back to her side. I pull her into a hug next. "But I love hugging Maddy the most!" I rock her back and forth and she tries to fight me off.

"You're being embarrassing again!" But she says this with a smile.

"Hey, we're still standing here," Chloe says, motioning to her and Charlie. She has her fingers intertwined with Charlie's; they look natural together, like their hands are meant to be like this.

"Sorry…" Maddy tries to apologize and pull away, but I just tighten my grip on her.

"I had to listen to your guy's lovey dovey talk, so I get to hold Maddy like this in front of you."

At this point Maddy can't stop smiling. It's like her lips are glued in a permanent upward position. Charlie rolls his eyes. It looks as though he wants to say something but a car pulls up behind him.

I was expecting his friend to look like a typical rocker guy, long hair and ripped jean jacket, but instead he seems like a modest guy, with short, straight brown hair and light brown eyes. He wears a blue collared shirt and plain jeans.

Charlie opens the back door for us. "This is Kevin, he's a guitarist and the lead singer for our band. He's a cool guy."

He raises three fingers to say hi. "Sup."

As we pile into the back seat, with me in the middle, Charlie introduces us. "Kev, this is my girlfriend Chloe, my sister Michelle, and my sister's girlfriend Maddy."

My corners of my lips curl upwards slightly when he calls me his sister, but even more when he refers to Maddy as my girlfriend.

"Girlfriend?" Kevin doesn't look disgusted, just curious.

"Yeah." I wasn't sure how he was going to react, but I wasn't going to deny anything.

He thinks for a bit but puts the car in drive and starts the ride. "That's cool" is all he says, and I decide there that I like and respect this guy.

"I'm excited to finally see you play!" Chloe is practically bouncing off her seat. This is probably a dream come true to her.

"Yeah, it's been a while since I heard you play." What Maddy says surprises me. I didn't think anyone heard him play. "You used to play all the time in elementary school and middle school, why did you ever stop?"

Maddy's question is innocent, a genuine question, but I see Charlie's jaw clench and his eyes look down, a dark memory coming up.

I don't want him to feel pressured. "Charlie you don't have to…"

"No, it's okay." He seems to have reached his resolve. He's finally ready to tell me everything.

"When I was in fifth grade, my mom bought me this expensive guitar, it was a fender CC-60S concert acoustic guitar with a sunburst finish." I nod like I understand what he's saying. "Mom signed me up for lessons in a town nearby, and that's when I met the other guys in the band."

"Although we didn't officially start a band until later." says Kevin.

"Yeah, anyway, as I got better I wanted to play for anyone who would listen, so for holidays or birthday parties I would play, and I got a lot of attention…and there was someone in my family who didn't like it when others got attention."

I flinch, knowing who he's talking about. My mind goes to a time Zach mentioned how he broke Charlie's guitar, and I realize where this story is headed.

"In eighth grade, me and some of the boys from the music school…"

"Including me!" Kevin chimes in.

"Yeah, we were asked to perform live at a school dance."

"Yeah, I remember that!" Maddy joins in.

"What? Why don't I remember?" Chloe asks.

"Oh…the dance was actually held for athletes…to celebrate the work we put in."

Chloe rolls her eyes. "Tsk, typical."

"Yeah, our middle school may have had a soft spot for the athletes, but that doesn't matter. What mattered was all of the girls were only paying attention to me."

Kevin glances over. "Don't you mean us?"

"Yeah, sure…anyway, when we got home that night, Zach was pissed. We got into a fight and it ended with Zach smashing my guitar." We all go silent. We knew that this was coming; it made sense knowing Zach.

"Well, I cried, and my mom and dad were pissed, especially my mom who spent a lot of money on that guitar. The music school sold us a cheap used guitar, but I didn't take it home. I was afraid Zach might smash that one, too."

"So he kept it at my house." says Kevin.

"I was also afraid to perform in front of people, at least while Zach was there, so if we did performances, it was at their school" He motions his head to Kevin.

"But even at our school he was shy, he wouldn't talk to anyone or take any photos."

"I was worried Zach would find out. But yeah, my mom said she would save up, and for my eighteenth birthday she would buy me an even better guitar." Sam's eyes sink and there's sorrow in his voice. "But obviously that didn't happen."

No one knows what to say, especially Chloe. Maddy looks guilty, like she somehow blames herself for Zach's behavior.

I remember another thing I heard from Paul. "Sam made you a guitar, right?"

Charlie slowly begins his story again. "Yeah. He remembered Mom's promise, so for our birthday this year he made me a guitar. He also gave it to me in secret so Zach wouldn't know."

"And he kept that one at my house, too!" sings Kevin.

Charlie sighs, annoyed. "Yes, and I kept it at your house. So yeah, if that answers your question, that's the reason why no one saw me play anymore." Once again, no one says anything. I don't want to say sorry to him since he's probably heard that before, and I don't want him to feel like we're pitying him. So I try to say something to lighten the mood.

"We should kill Zach."

"No." Charlie responds immediately. "We're not doing that."

Maddy begins chuckling and eventually Chloe and I join in. Charlie smiles and shakes his head. "I mean, to be honest, Maddy, you breaking up with him basically killed him, and then going to Michelle put the nail in the coffin." He looks back at her. "I thank you for that."

Maddy shrugs like it isn't a big deal "Yeah, I mean, it's no problem, he was the worst so…"

We pull up to a modest-looking house, a simple two story, but not as big as the Owens'es house. The garage is open and we see a drum set, amps, and two other people inside. Getting out of the car, we head over to meet the group. The two boys look up and greet Charlie. One boy looks to be the same age as Kevin and Charlie. He has buzzed hair and a lip piercing. Charlie introduces us. "This is Axel, our drummer."

He nods with a "Sup."

The other boy is fiddling around with a bass guitar. He looks much younger than the rest of the boys, like he's only in his freshman year. He's short with strawberry blond hair and freckles. "And this is Christian."

He gives a sweet "Hi," and goes back to tuning.

Kevin puts his arm around Charlie's neck. "And this is Charlie, he does electric guitar."

"Electric, I thought you did acoustic?" Maddy asks, since she's only ever seen him play the acoustic.

"Yeah, but then my asshole brother broke my acoustic guitar and the next one I got was electric."

"Oh right, sorry."

Kevin gets us chairs to sit on while the boys finish setting up. Chloe looks around excitedly. "So, what's your band's name?"

Kevin responds, "We're Harvey's Band."

"Harvey's Band?" Chloe looks a little put off by the name.

"Yeah, who's Harvey?" I would think that if they chose someone's name it would be one of theirs.

"Harvey's the name of the music school we met at, so we're Harvey's Band," Charlie says, finishing the tuning of his guitar.

Chloe gets excited again. "Aww, that's cute, I like it!"

"It's not supposed to sound cute, it's supposed to sound cool." the drummer says, seeming oddly offended.

"Yeah, yeah, sure it does… It's totally cool, dude." Kevin says as he slings his guitar over his shoulder. "Shall we get practicing?"

The boys start. Their genre is sort of punk rock, their sound reminding me of Nirvana or Radiohead, and they're actually really good. After each song they play, Chloe springs up and cheers. Maddy and I sit and clap, but I'm also very impressed.

Kevin speaks into the mic, like he's addressing a crowd. "And for this last number, I'm going to hand the microphone to our electric guitarist, Charlie, who has a special song for a special lady." Chloe looks stunned so Maddy and I cheer.

Charlie steps in the front, face bright red, and takes the microphone. "Umm, I wrote this song for you Chloe, I hope you enjoy it." Charlie takes a deep breath, his hands trembling as he starts singing.

Charlie has a surprisingly sweet voice, his voice reminding me of something you would hear in a school choir, like he would be the kid that would get the solo performance. The lyrics go:

Trapped in a box,

I can't find my way,

I look towards a light, but all I can see is your face,

Red, like a fire, warm, like a ray,

I fought through the shower, but only saw rain.

You brought out the sun, you brought out the day,

You tried to make it stop, you tried to fight the pain,

But we can't do it alone,

There's already way too much,

I just need you to stand by me,

I only need your touch.

As he finishes the lyrics, he keeps playing and says, "Chloe… Thank you for listening to me, and thank you for staying at my side. You help me more than you know… Will you be my date to homecoming?"

I see tears in Chloe's eyes as she gets up, covering her mouth, and runs to Charlie, wrapping her arms around his neck. "Yes, yes, I will!" The boys in the band all cheer and clap, and Maddy and I do, too.

Maddy leans over to me. "When you ask me, it better be this cute."

"Who said I'm asking you?"

"What? You don't want to go with me?" Maddy says in a teasing manner. She knows I'd want to go with her…if I wanted to go.

"I like you, but I don't like school dances, I find them boring, Also…people are going to stare at us…,"

"And?"

"And I don't like people looking at me."

"You should go! I'll be there, and Sam and Charlie will be there!" Maddy's face was full of determination.

"And Zach will be there…"

"Well, screw him!" I'm not going to budge. "Maddy, sorry, sweetie, but you're not winning this." Maddy looks away in thought, but it seems like she finds a loophole. "Charlie!"

Charlie looks up from his Chloe embrace. "What?"

"I can talk to some teachers and get your band to play at homecoming!" *Oh no, I see where this is going…*

"I don't know. What about…"

"That was in the past! And also, Zach already lost, he won't try anything."

Chloe gets on board with the idea. "She's right, babe! You would look so hot up there! You could stick it to Zach, tell him you're still playing guitar and you're still better than him."

Oh god, Chloe, don't encourage him.

"Yeah, man, we're tired of only playing at our school! Let's do this."

Charlie gives in. "Okay, okay, fine, we can play at my school."

Everyone starts patting Charlie on the back and Chloe gives him a kiss. Maddy crosses her arms and looks at me with a smug smile.

"Ugh, fine, Maddy, will you go to homecoming with me?"

Her smile turns sweet. "Yes. Don't worry, it'll be a lot of fun!"

Chapter 21

"This is not fun." I sit on the floor of Maddy's room with a frown while she curls my hair.

"It'll be lots of fun! Especially with Charlie's band playing!" Chloe is getting her makeup done by Sasha, who is creating a stunning look for her.

Maddy invited us girls to her home to get ready. I was nervous going to her house this time, since her parents would be home.

"Did you tell your parents…you know, about us?"

"Of course!" Maddy's response is so chipper I thought she didn't hear the question correctly.

"Wait, actually?"

"Yeah, I tell my parents everything." I feel a pang in my heart. I had almost forgotten that most people have normal parents that actually talk to them.

"They're not ashamed or anything?"

"No, they're actually happy that I broke up with Zach. It seems everyone but me could see how bad he was for me."

"Meh, love makes you blind, literally, not just a saying."

We all do a little fashion show for each other.

Chloe's dress is puffy, short, and pink. It is a delightful confection, featuring layers of tulle that give it a playful and feminine flair. She flips her dark red hair back and forth, showing off the perfect curls.

Sasha wears a more down-to-earth dress. Just a dark blue spaghetti strap number that goes to her knees. The dark color makes her orange hair pop even more.

Maddy's dress is stunning, but to me she looks stunning in everything. It's a long velvety red dress. It exudes elegance, its rich fabric gracefully flowing with a luxurious sheen, creating a timeless and sophisticated silhouette. She tries to be modest while posing, but we all know she looks the best.

I'm next, sporting a six-dollar dress I found at Goodwill. It's short, to my thighs, and strapless, a little sexier than I usually wear. It's a white dress with shining gold flowers on it and a big gold bow on the chest area.

"Wooow, look at this sexy lady." I roll my eyes in embarrassment. Maddy is clearly teasing me like when I told her she was sexy.

"Everyone looks so pretty! We're going to grab everyone's attention," Chloe says as she examines herself in the mirror.

"God, I hope not..."

We hear a knock on the bedroom door.

"Hello? Are there four little ladies in here done getting ready?"

"Mom!"

A sweet wholesome giggle is heard, and a beautiful woman who looks to be in her fifties opens the door. She has the same blonde hair as Maddy with browning roots. Her dark blue eyes immediately land on me.

"Oh! You must be Michelle! Ohhh, let me come give you a hug!" The bubbly woman shuffles over to me and pulls me into a tight hug. I can smell the elegance radiating off of her thick perfume.

I become stiff when she hugs me. I'm not used to being hugged by adults, not even Paul ever hugs me.

Maddy must notice my discomfort. "Mom, stop! You're making her uncomfortable!"

"Oh, am I?" She immediately lets go. "Sorry about that, sweetie, I'm just so excited to meet you!" I'm overwhelmed by the amount of energy her mom has, so I'm not able to really respond to her, just a, "Yeah…" which is barely heard over her yelling, "*Honey*, get in here and meet Michelle!"

I can barely handle meeting her mother so I'm worried about her father, and I was right to be worried—he's basically a carbon copy of the mom, just with dark hair and a mustache.

Matching her energy, he waltzes right up to me and grabs my hand. "Michelle! Oh, it's so great to meet you! Oh, we've heard so much about you!" I am once again overwhelmed by the meeting.

"You know we are so thankful to you, I never liked that Zach boy." Her mom comes to my side and gossips like we're best friends. "He gave me a bad feeling."

"Mhm, I agree, I didn't like how he treated my baby girl. Felt like he had her on a leash or something." Maddy hides her face in her hands at her dad's comment.

Her mom continues, "But of course our little Maddy praised him, saying he was the 'love of her life' and we only want our little princess to be happy."

"Mom, stop, you're embarrassing me!" Maddy stomps her foot down, her face red from shame.

"Oh, hush now, sweetheart! That's all in the past. Now I want to meet Michelle. So Michelle, how long have you been a lesbian for?"

"Mom! Oh my god, it's not like she's a vegetarian! You don't just wake up and decide you're a lesbian." I actually find it amusing to see Maddy get to worked up. Usually when I tease her she tries to play it off cool or tease me back, but it's fun to see her true flustered reactions.

"I know what a lesbian is, calm down." She faces me again. "You know, my brother who lives in California, he's gay. Of course we were all shocked at first, but he's still my brother and nothing is going to change that."

"Wow, I really appreciate that." It's good to know that Maddy's mother is one of those people that sees past sexuality. A lot of people have trouble with that, so it makes me feel more comfortable with her.

"For me, as long as my daughter is with someone who will treat her right, then I'm okay with them." Her father smiles at me. "And that boy Zach did not treat my little princess right." Maddy once again hides her face.

"I promise, Mr. Vitis, I also want Maddy to be happy. She's the most amazing girl I've ever met." I hear Maddy's mom say, "Aww," in the background and her dad just brings me into a hug.

"I knew you were a good one, and you can call me Alex."

"Oh and call me Laurie!" Her mom pops up in front of my face. "And I just want you to know, if you ever need a place, you are welcome here."

"Just keep those doors open, okay?" Her dad laughs proudly at his joke while Maddy groans.

I'm touched by what they say—the idea of actual supportive parents is foreign to me. "Thank you both for that."

Alex pats me on the head. "No, we should be thanking you, really!"

"Now, girls." Laurie motions to Sasha and Chloe. "Let's get together for some group photos!" She pulls out her phone and Maddy groans some more. "Come on, come on, this is the first time you've had friends over in a while."

I look at Maddy, shocked. "Really?"

"Yeah, I mean, I never really trusted my 'friends,' so I didn't want them at my house."

I remember how her 'friends' treated her. "Right, sorry…"

She shakes her head. "It's fine, I like you guys way better." She puts her hands on my waist and pulls me close for the iconic "prom pose." She whispers in my ear, "Smile." I feel my face heat up as I give a shy smile.

We take about a hundred photos, Alex and Laurie hyping us up for everyone. We do group photos in all sorts of poses and jumps, and then Maddy and I do a few shots of just the two of us. Eventually it gets dark out and Maddy pushes us out the door. "Mom! Dad! We have to go or we'll be late!"

"Oh, just one more picture!"

"*No!*" Maddy slams the door shut and stomps to her car.

I catch up to her right away. "Your parents are sweet, I like them a lot."

"Ugh, please, they're so embarrassing."

"There are worse things parents can be than embarrassing." My eyes widen at the realization of what I just said. That was a thought inside my head that I accidentally said out loud. Maddy looks down, with a fake smile hiding her embarrassment. "Wait, Maddy, I…"

"No, it's okay, you're right, and I do remember you saying you didn't have the best relationship with your family, so I know I shouldn't complain."

I don't want her to feel that way, so I pull her in for a hug and reassure her, "You can feel embarrassed by your parents, there's nothing wrong with that."

She relaxes into me. "Yeah, I know."

"Come on, you love birds, let's get this show on the road! My boyfriend's going to be on stage tonight!" Chloe runs past us to the car, as Sasha slugs behind.

I sigh. "I'm totally not going to have fun at this dance…"

"You totally are."

***

I totally did not. The music is loud, it's hot, and I keep being pushed around by the crowd. Maddy looks like she's having fun, though, so I guess that makes it worth it.

I also get to meet the boy Sasha has been crushing on. He's muscular with dirty brown hair and dark brown eyes. I guess Sasha has a thing for muscular guys. She told me they "have multiple classes together" and got close that way. She spends most of the dance with him, except for a few special songs she dances with us. They both look awkward and inexperienced with each other, but that has this cute charm attached to it. I don't know if their relationship will grow, but I'll leave that decision to Sasha.

I spend my time with Chloe, Charlie, Maddy, and Sam. Sam says he's there as my bodyguard, to protect me in case Zach does anything. I see Zach, his arms all over a new girl. I recognize her from the cheer team.

"That's Johanna, a junior who's been crushing on Zach since her freshman year. She must be jumping with joy to be his partner." Maddy has a bit of sass at the last part. She doesn't seem jealous, just annoyed.

"I honestly feel bad for the girl; she hasn't realized how much he sucks yet."

"Hopefully she figures it out soon and dumps him."

"Yeah, if she's lucky."

The music slows down and everyone partners up. Sam comes over and whispers in my ear, "I'll be on standby in case anything happens." As he walks away, he puts his finger to his ear as if he has an earpiece on. I chuckle watching him make sure the coast is clear.

I feel Maddy's arms wrap around my neck and I instinctively wrap my arms around her waist.

I get close to her and whisper, "You know, this is my first time slow dancing."

She responds with a flirtatious tone, "Really? I would have never known."

As we spin around together, I examine the room. I see Chloe with her face buried in Charlie's chest, and Charlie resting his head on Chloe's. I believe this is the last number before he needs to go backstage to set up with his band. I see the two boys who came out as gay to me in the lunch room dancing together. They either like each other or are dancing together because they're the only gays at school. I believe in the former. After a while I begin to notice people staring at us. My blood goes cold and I feel a shiver down my spine.

Maddy whispers to me, "What's wrong?"

"People are staring…"

She snuggles her head on mine. "Who cares, let them."

"I just get freaked out by attention…"

"Then focus on something else…"

As I notice more and more people staring, my anxiety gets worse. "I can't."

"Then focus on this." Maddy grabs my chin and presses her lips onto mine, catching me by surprise with the sudden public kiss. I am stiff at first, but feeling Maddy's lips melt into mine

I begin to relax, and fully appreciate the kiss. As we release, I find us alone in the gym. We are the only people in the room, probably the world, and I don't care. All I need is Maddy in front of me.

I wish the song could last forever and we would be permanently stuck in the moment, but the song ends, and Charlie bids us farewell to go set up with his band. Chloe frowns as she waves him off.

"Come on, guys, let's make our way front and center." Maddy looks around. "Where's Sasha?"

Sam joins us and we find Sasha and her date. The six of us make our way to the front. It's a good ten minutes before they start, so we stand and dance by the stage.

Soon the lights drop and the curtains open, revealing Charlie and his band under blinding lights. Chloe screams as Kevin introduced them. "We are Harvey's Band! Thank you for having us!" I hear a silent "One.. Two…" and they are off, jamming away.

It takes a while for the crowd to get into it, but Chloe is going crazy the entire time. "Whoo! That's my boyfriend! That's my boyfriend!" She points at Charlie while jumping up and down.

Sam is standing next to me, nodding and stomping his feet to the sound.

I get close to him to whisper, "I heard you made that guitar."

"That's right, Charlie tell you?"

"Actually Paul… It looks nice."

"Thanks, I knew how upset he would be after the promise Mom made him, so I asked for some help and figured out how to make it for him."

"It's beautiful, the red color really makes it stand out."

"The two of us have been overshadowed by Zach for so long, I wanted to give him something to make him seen."

When Sam mentions Zach's name, I scan the crowd to see if I can find him, worried about what he might do to Charlie. I don't see him, and I don't know if that's a good thing or a bad thing. Even if he does try something, we won't let him.

Watching Charlie play up on the stage is the happiest I've ever seen him. His passion for music radiates with each note, and the crowd's applause echoes the joy in his heart.

Charlie plays his heart out for the hour long set, and the crowd goes wild. Chloe explodes, and I feel like a proud mom. After they finish, all of the members come off stage and people swarm them, especially Charlie.

"Oh my god, Charlie! I didn't know you played! You're so good!"

"Do you guys do shows anywhere else?"

"Should I get your autograph before you're famous!"

Multiple girls are overwhelming Charlie. He looks to us for help as Chloe stands next to me pouting. I nudge her forward. "Go to him."

She turns her face away. "Why should I, he has plenty of girls around him."

I laugh and turn her face to look at him. "Does he look happy?" Charlie is backing up from the crowd, panic in his eyes, laughing nervously. "You're his girlfriend, go save him."

Chloe shakes off her nerves. "You're right, why am I just standing here being jealous? I'm going to go introduce myself as his girlfriend." Chloe pushes through the crowd and nuzzles herself next to Charlie, which he responds to by putting an arm around her shoulder and pulling her close.

"This is my girlfriend, Chloe."

"Hi, I'm his girlfriend, Chloe." The group girls of surrounding Charlie look disappointed and walk away.

"Thanks for that, babe, they were getting way too close." He kisses her on the head.

"No problem! But *oh my god, you were so good*!" Chloe is back to jumping up and down and being a proper groupie of the band.

I turn to Maddy, "Okay, I danced, I socialized, I saw Charlie play, am I allowed to leave now?"

Maddy smiles. "Fine." She pats my head. "You did a very good job tonight."

I push her hand off. "Uh huh…" I grab her hand and start leading her to the door. "Let's go."

She giggles as I pull her. "Wait, we need to say goodbye."

"Ugh." I turn around to where Sam, Sasha, and Chloe are standing with Charlie and his band and shout, "BYE BITCHES." They look at me confused at first but eventually wave me goodbye. "Alright, now we can go."

I hear Maddy's light giggles as we head towards the door. We're almost there when I feel a pair of eyes burning a hole in my chest. I turn to face the hostile stare, and it's Zach. Standing at the back of the room, with that girl still clinging to him, his eyes are sharp, deprived of warmth, and reveal a deeply hidden rage. My body goes cold.

"What's wrong?" Maddy bumps into me with a curious expression. I don't want her to see Zach so I force a smile. "Nothing, let's go."

I need to get Zach out of my mind. He isn't worthy of my thoughts, plus tonight will be the first sleepover I've had since middle school. We got Maddy's parents' permission and now I get to spend the night with Maddy.

"So, did you end up having any fun?"

"Hmm, well, I liked dancing with you, and I liked hearing Charlie play…so I guess it wasn't that bad."

Her face beams. "Great, so we can do it again for prom!"

"Oh no…" I hide my head in my hand, knowing there is no avoiding it this time.

"But for prom I better get a real promposal, okay?"

I chuckle. "I will make it the most grand promposal at the school, will that work?"

She gives me a winning smile and flips her hair. "Yes, it does."

When we make it back to her house, her parents are still up watching TV.

Her mom pops her head up. "Wow, you two made it back early!"

"Too excited for your sleepover?"

"Dad!" Both her parents let out loud laughs. "We came home early because Michelle doesn't like dances."

"Regretfully, me and school functions don't mix well."

"Well then, why don't you come join us for a bit, we're watching *Alien*! A classic." Her mom motions with her hand for us to sit.

Maddy looks at me for my opinion and I shrug. "I like scary movies."

So, we join her parents. I enjoy watching their reactions to the movie more than the actual movie. Her mom screams out loud at every jump scare and her dad complains about her scream scaring him. Everyone laughs together, creating a heartwarming atmosphere that I'm not used to, but enjoy.

After the movie is over Maddy and I lie awake in her bed, just having a peaceful conversation.

"Your family is really nice."

"They're embarrassing, but I guess they're alright."

"It's good they support you."

"Yeah, I was surprised. They were shocked at first, but they asked if I was sure I really liked you and eventually came to accept it." We lie together with our legs tangled, our heartbeats matching, and our breaths close. I had come to realize there was something I hadn't asked Maddy yet.

"By the way...what is your sexuality?"

Maddy looks up with a little, "Huh?"

"Like, do you think you're a lesbian?"

"Oh...I don't know...I mean, I definitely did like Zach."

"Then maybe bi?

Maddy's eyebrows scrunch with a puzzled expression as she thinks hard about it. "I don't know. I mean, I like you...but you're the only girl I seem to like, so maybe I'm Michellesexual?" She looks at me with a smirk.

The comment earns a light laugh from me. "You don't need to know now, you can figure it out later."

"Just like figuring everything else out later?"

My face is pensive and my lips purse as I think of the answer. "Yeah."

Maddy smiles. "Anything else you wanna know?"

"Do you have any siblings?

"No, you?"

"Nope."

Maddy looks at me with upturned eyebrows and a slight frown. "What about your parents?"

"What about my parents?"

"I know you said you don't have a very good relationship with them."

"I have a very awful relationship with them." I say it in a point blank manner, but I probably should have held back a little.

"Right." I watch Maddy, waiting for the next question. "Do you wanna talk about it?"

I roll over to face the ceiling. "Not a lot to talk about. My dad's abusive, my mom wouldn't do anything, and I felt like it was a dream come true when they said I didn't have to live with them for my senior year "

"Have they tried calling you?"

"My mom has, but I barely tell her anything, just that I'm alive and keeping up with my homework."

"So they know you don't want to go to college?"

"Nope."

"Do they know you're a lesbian?"

"Yep."

Maddy snuggles closer to me. "You know you can always talk to me, right?"

I turn and cuddle into her. "I know."

Her voice begins to get more hushed as she starts to drift to sleep. "And my parents, too, they like you."

"Mmhmm."

Maddy's breathing becomes heavier and she drifts to sleep. I kiss her forehead and whisper, "Thank you," before falling asleep myself.

Chapter 22

I hear a soft knock coming from my door as I'm getting ready.

"Come in!"

Paul peeks his head in. "Who's ready for their big day?" He comes in with a bouquet of flowers.

I cover my mouth. "Oh my god, Paul, you didn't have to get me flowers!"

"What? Can't I be proud that the young girl I'm housing has a painting in an art museum?"

I smile. Today is the day, the opening of the new exhibit with my painting in it. There will be a small ceremony as they reveal the paintings one at a time. All my friends are getting ready to go to the viewing, as are Paul and Maddy's parents. It makes me feel honored that so many people are going to be there to support me.

"That's a beautiful dress," Paul says as he gives me the flowers.

"Thanks, Maddy got it for me for Christmas, I promised her I'd wear it today."

Maddy got me a beautiful silky dress the color of a pearl. It goes to my ankles and has short puffy sleeves. The top of the dress is black and a bow with a diamond in the center lays on the bust.

Without knowing, we both got each other clothes. Maddy said she wanted to prove to herself that she knew my style. I got her a pale blue leather jacket I found since I wanted to prove the same to her.

"I love it! I love leather jackets, they're so chic."

I giggled. "I know, and unlike some people I know your favorite color."

She scoffed. "Oh, you…but I love it! I'll wear it on the day of the exhibit if you wear the dress I got you."

"I was going to wear it regardless so don't worry, it's gorgeous."

"I'm glad. By the way, how is Zach…like at home? Has he caused you any trouble?"

"With Paul and the boys there, no…he's actually been really quiet. It's like I never see him anymore."

"Well, that's good right?"

"I don't know…I feel nervous not knowing where he is."

That hasn't changed since Christmas. It's almost like he's toying with me, like he's hiding from me on purpose, just to psychologically torture me.

I'm constantly worrying about if he might try or do anything, so he's always on my mind, but I think that's his goal, he wants me to be scared. But I won't let him get the better of me, especially not today.

Maddy mentioned that her parents would be taking Chloe, Sasha, and her to the museum. Meanwhile Paul will be driving Sam, Charlie, and me. The fact that I'll have eight people there to support me is like something from a dream. It's surreal and heartwarming, but it could all end at the drop of a hat.

"We'll be waiting for you downstairs." Seeing Paul's reassuring smile wakes me up to reality. I really do have that many people that want to be there for me, and although I may think I don't always deserve it, Maddy taught me that it's okay to be a little greedy sometimes.

I do one more check in the mirror and head out. Sam, Charlie, and Paul are waiting downstairs for me. As they see me, they begin to applaud, which is mortifying.

"What are you guys doing?"

"What? This is a big day for you!" Paul snaps a photo of me.

"You're acting like I'm graduating or getting married."

Sam consoled me, "Achieving your goal in life is way more important than graduating or getting married."

 I can't argue against him on this one. To me, this is way bigger than if I was graduating, but still a little too much for me. I nudge him. "Does that mean we should celebrate for you once you send out your shipment?"

"Wait, hold on, we're talking about you right now, not me." Sam has been busy working on the furniture for the cafe order. His deadline is the end of February and he's about 75 percent done with the work, so he's taking his time.

"Well, when my band books its first paying gig, I want an even bigger celebration than this." As I think of us giving flowers and cheering Charlie on, I laugh. Of course I want to see Charlie's band grow, but seeing Charlie come down the stairs holding flowers as we all clap is straight up hilarious.

"Well, if you're all ready, then let's get a move on." We piled out of the house and I do a quick 360 to see if I can spot Zach anywhere. I could ask Paul where Zach is, but then I'd be giving Zach what he wants, which is me worrying about him. So I hold my tongue and get in the car.

As the boys fight over the aux cord, I gaze out the window, watching the trees and fields speed by. I'm reminded of the first time I drove in Paul's car. It was almost four months ago when a shy teen was picked up by a man she'd never met. I thought I'd have a quiet year away from my parents, but I didn't know I'd end up with genuine friends, a real father figure, and most surprisingly, a girlfriend.

I also never thought I would actually see one of my paintings hang in a museum. I always figured I'd go like Van Gogh, dying alone, my art only being recognized after I die, but here I am at eighteen, going to see an exhibit featuring my gay art.

I don't remember much of the ride. I'm in a trance of nervousness and excitement the whole time, but I think Sam and Charlie go back and forth with the music. It's a Saturday, so the museum is busier than usual, but it's a small museum in a small city, so it's not crowded like the Philly art museum.

I see other kids who look my age with their parents. They are pointing at photos and fixing their appearances, probably the other kids whose pieces got picked. They also look as nervous as me, which makes me feel a lot better. It's reassuring to know I'm not the only one freaking out.

"Michi!" Chloe shouts to grab my attention. She's on her toes waving hysterically at me, wearing the biggest grin I've seen her have.

Paul nudges Charlie with his elbow. "That's your girlfriend, right?"

Charlie blushes and gives a shy smile. "Yeah."

"She's pretty." Paul flashes a thumbs-up. "I approve."

"Dad!"

"And that's your girlfriend over there." Paul lightly pushes me forward towards Maddy.

A gleeful smile appears on my lips as I watch Maddy stomp towards me, her heels clicking with each step and her hair flowing behind her. She wears the jacket that I got her with a floral patterned dress.

It's like the first time I saw and fell for her. "Yeah, that's my girlfriend." I can say it proudly this time.

"Hi."

"Hi…are you going to threaten me to stay away from your boyfriend?"

I catch Maddy off guard. "Pfft, what?" The realization crosses her face. "Oh my god, don't bring that up."

"Hehehe." I wrap my arms around Maddy. "Teasing you is the best part of the day."

"Well, the best part of *today* should be revealing your painting."

I smirk and whisper to her ear, "Are you sure you're not just excited for everyone to see *your* painting?"

Maddy blushes and pushes me off playfully. "You!"

"Hey, you two, I thought we agreed to leave the doors open." Maddy's dad steps between us, using his arm like a barrier. Maddy rolls her eyes in embarrassment, but I think it's cute.

"Oh, Michelle!" Maddy's mom comes and gives me a hug but immediately lets go. "Right, almost forgot, you're not a hugger."

"It's okay, umm, thank you for coming."

"Of course! Anyone who makes our Maddy happy is a friend to us!"

I laugh with Lauri Vitis. Like Maddy, she has very infectious laughter; it brings you in even if you don't want it.

Out of the corner of my eye, I see Paul approach Maddy. "Hello, Maddy, long time no see."

"Hi, Mr. Owens." Maddy is very polite with him. "How have you been?"

"I've been good, thank you." The two are very rigid and professional with each other, not at all relaxed. The last time Maddy met Paul she was Zach's girlfriend. So it must be awkward to see him again. And Paul must feel bad for how his son treated her, so overall it's an awkward reunion.

"Umm, hi. Nice to meet you, Mr. Owens." Chloe stands next to Maddy and shyly introduces herself, not even looking him in the eyes.

He lets out a booming laugh. "Yes, you're Chloe, right? Thank you for taking care of my dumbass son."

"Hey!"

"Oh, please, you're barely passing. We'll be lucky if you graduate."

Chloe laughs awkwardly, still too shy to relax. She is trying her best not to make a bad impression.

"You can relax, Chloe, don't feel you need to impress me or anything." Paul then turns to Maddy and puts his hand on her shoulder. "Maddy, try not to be a stranger, okay?"

Maddy looks up with hope in her eyes. A soft smile appears across her lips as she takes in Paul's words.

I enjoy watching the interaction between Paul and the girls, but my attention is taken away when I feel a fragile tap on my shoulder. I turn and am speechless.

"Ms. Park? What…what are you doing here?" I'm genuinely surprised. She hasn't mentioned the exhibit to me once since we learned my piece got picked.

"Can an art teacher not see her student's art being revealed in a museum?" Ms. Park sounds the same as she always does, monotone and unconcerned.

"Yes, sorry, thank you for coming." I'm bewildered by the sight. Ms. Park nods with a blank stare and wanders off to the exhibit hall.

"I told you she cares." Sasha pops up from behind, startling me. She recently dyed her hair white, and wears pale pink lipstick today. I didn't freak out this time when I saw the change.

"Yeah, it's weird, she's the last person I thought would show up.

Sasha smiles. "She must have taken a liking to you."

I am once again confused. "But…I haven't done anything."

She shrugs. "Then I guess she really likes your art."

"I hate to interrupt this guys"—Sam's strong arms wrap around our shoulders—"but I think it's time for the revealing."

As I notice the other students have disappeared, the panic starts to come back—what if everyone hates it? Ms. Park and Sasha are artists so they will be able to pinpoint any mistakes. I feel like I'm going to throw up, but Maddy appears beside me and grabs my hand.

"They're gonna love it." She squeezes my hand and I squeeze it back and we walk hand in hand to the exhibit hall.

We watch as each painting is revealed. The student artist stands at the front and says a few words about it. We were told in advance that we would have to say a line or two so Maddy helped me practice. I feel very confident about saying two things in front of like ten strangers. I'm most worried about my painting not being good compared to others.

Most of the other students' works are abstract and experimental paintings. Each artist has their own unique perspective on the world, using bold strokes and strong hues to convey their stories. All of the students stumble on their words, but they stand proud when they hear the "oohs" and "ahhs" of the crowd.

I watch as we get closer and closer to my painting. The crowd shrinks after each painting is revealed, most likely due to parents wanting to stay and admire only their child's artwork, which means they are only about three people I don't know when the time comes for my painting to be revealed.

Maddy holds my hand as my name and school are announced. I take a deep breath and walk to the front. My friends are all watching with eager faces, ready to see the creation I have been slaving over for weeks. The last thing I notice are tears in Ms. Park's eyes. She stands silently to the side, tall and proud, a wide closed mouth smile plastered across her face, and she has tears. Tears of joy for her student, tears to show how proud she is. I feel very touched. Ms. Park gives me the last bit of courage I need to go up there.

"Hello. My name is Michelle and for my senior year of high school, I was told that I would be moving from the familiar streets of Philadelphia, to the unknown valleys of a small town in Ohio. I love to paint beautiful things, so I painted the most beautiful thing I saw in Ohio. Thank you."

I step aside and let the current fall from the painting. I close my eyes, not wanting to see anyone's reaction, until I hear the soft gasps and tears of the crowd. I open my eyes to see mouths wide open and tears streaming down their cheeks.

"That's our baby girl!" Laurie says as she sobs silently into a tissue.

Alex has just as many tears as his wife. "It really is!" They pull Maddy in for a hug as I hear them say, "Did you know about this?"

The Owens family stands there with their mouths hung open.

"Who knew we had someone this talented living under our roof!" Paul looks up with stars in his eyes.

"I mean, I'm a pretty talented musician. Oww!" Sam elbows Charlie in the side to shut him up.

The tears that were starting to form in Ms. Park's eyes are now streaming down her face, and for the first time ever, I see her teeth. She has a large grin, the size of her entire face, and she lightly applauds my piece.

"Michi!" Chloe and Sasha run over and hug me! "I'm so proud of..." Chloe stops mid-sentence, and the look on her face is that of terror, like all the blood is draining from it.

"What is it?" I turn and go cold. Zach is walking in, with an evil grin on his face. As everyone takes note of my horrid expression, they all turn and see him. Maddy's parents back away and hold Maddy tight in their arms. Chloe and Sasha step in front of me and the Owens step in front of Zach.

Charlie pushes Zach back. "What the hell are you doing here?"

"Hold on, Charlie." Paul puts his arm up to stop Charlie from getting any more aggressive, but Zach just laughs.

"What? I can't enjoy the art show, too?"

Paul's eyebrows narrow and his voice gets low. "Zach, you know very well you weren't invited."

Zach begins to argue with Paul. "But it's a public place!" I just stand there frozen in fear, trying to process if this is really happening.

Zach's eyes meet mine and I stumble back. Maddy runs right to my side after that. "Don't worry, Michelle, I won't let him hurt you."

I'm barely focusing on what Maddy is saying, I just keep seeing Zach's smile. *Why is he smiling?* Something isn't right.

"Son, you need to leave, do *NOT* start this now!" Although he's keeping his voice low, I can hear the aggression in Paul's voice.

"But Dad, I'm just here dropping off some guests…" Zach motions towards the door. "They flew in just for this." Zach's spine-chilling smile never leaves.

Everyone's gazes go to the door, and a large pit opens in my stomach. I feel the hair on my body start to stand up and a chill goes down my spine. My breathing becomes so loud that the voices around me sound muffled.

"Sweetie," my mother's soft voice squeaks out. She reaches out to hug me, but I step away. "Oh right…sorry…it's just so nice to see you." My mom is a fragile woman, skin and bones with dark circles under her eyes. I believe she's a coward.

My body shakes as my father walks right past me and up to my painting. "What the hell is this?"

The familiar sound of his voice makes me jump, like it always has. His already red, angry face won't even acknowledge me. "Uh…it's…" My voice is shaky; I can barely speak.

"Sweetheart, calm down." My mom goes to my father's side, as she always has.

Fear is building up in me, but as I come to accept the situation, my fear turns to anger. I look at Zach who is being yelled at by his dad. He stands there with the same shit-eating grin. Disgust boils in me—to think he would go this far over losing a girl.

I wait until he looks at me again. "Really? You brought my parents into this?" I am absolutely appalled by his actions. I didn't think he would ever sink this low. I can't understand how someone raised by the sweetest man could end up so rotten.

"Hey, I'm still talking to you." My father grabs my dress collar and pulls me in. "What have I told you about painting?"

When in the face of my father, I can't speak. "I…"

"It's not a real job and you need to focus on something actually useful in life! Stop ruining yourself with this meaningless shit." The more he talks, the more cracks I feel forming. "And what the hell is this…" He goes back to the painting. "A girl? Are you still having those thoughts?"

"No…I…"

"Oh, sir, that's a painting of your daughter's girlfriend, that's her over there!" Zach points towards Maddy who has a worried look on her face. Her parents shield her as Sam slams Zach up against the wall by the neck.

"I swear if you say one more thing…"

Paul grabs Sam's hand. "Calm down, son…"

Zach laughs in Sam's face. "Yeah, listen to Dad, like you always do!"

Paul's face turns a shade of red I've never seen, his veins basically popping out. "You listen…"

"Girlfriend?" My heart freezes. I see my father's face and I know what is going to happen next. There's nothing I can do, I'm powerless at this point. So I only close my eyes and take it.

No matter how many times, the punch still hurts. As I fall to the ground, something in me snaps, and I wake up from the dream. This is my reality, this is the life I'm supposed to live.

"*NO DAUGHTER OF MINE* IS GOING TO BE ONE OF THOSE HOMOSEXUALS!" My father is about to go in for another hit but my mom and even Paul rush in to stop him.

"George…has this been the type of person you've always been?" Paul was is in disbelief of my dad as he pushes him back.

"I'm disappointed in you, Paul. The only reason I sent her to you was in hopes your sons would put her on the right path! You have three of them, at least one should have made her stop having these…disgusting thoughts!"

Paul pushes George away. "The only thing disgusting is you! I can't believe I considered you a friend!"

"Excuse me?"

It's like I'm in the audience again, watching a play unfold before me. This time, the play is a tragedy. I watch my father and Paul argue, I watch as Chloe and Sasha tries to stop Sam and Charlie from hitting Zach, and I watch Maddy's face grow concerned for me, but there's nothing I can do.

"George, you need to…" My mom tries pleading with him, but he just pushes her away.

"No! Sending her here was a mistake! I should have just taken her to Germany with us. If she came with us she wouldn't be doing all this"—he walks to my painting—"this shit!" He grabs my painting and kicks a hole right through the canvas, absolutely destroying the painting I spent weeks on.

But I'm not surprised. I'm not someone who gets to have a dream. I'm someone who hides away, someone who is scared of her own shadow. Watching everyone fight over me, I can't take it, I can't do anything! So I just run. Like I've always done, run away and hide.

Chapter 23

Once upon a time, there was a little girl who liked to paint.

"Daddy! Daddy! Look! I painted you!"

"Haha, very cute, sweetie."

As the little girl got older, she kept painting.

"Daddy, my painting got a prize! Look!"

"That's nice, but you should focus more on your studies than your art. I mean look, a C- in math? Absolutely unacceptable."

But the girl didn't stop, she only got better and better.

"Hey Mom, Dad, can I go take art lessons after school? There's an academy nearby that offers lessons four times a week."

The girl's mother tried to speak up, but the father wouldn't let her.

"Absolutely not."

"But…"

"We're not going to waste money on something you'll never use."

"But…I wanna be a famous painter when I grow up!"

The father slammed his fists down on the table.

"Absolutely not! Painting isn't a job! You need to focus on something real. This art stuff is probably the reason why you're failing most of your classes! Forget after school art lessons, we're signing you up for math tutoring."

"But I hate math!"

"THEN LEARN TO LOVE IT!"

So the girl kept it a secret. She kept painting, but she wouldn't tell her father, she knew what would happen if she did. She hid her art and her passion away.

***

Once upon a time there was a young woman who realized she preferred women over men, but the young woman knew better than to let her father know, so she kept it a secret. But secrets are hard to keep.

"Michelle, get in here."

"Yes, Father?"

"I got a call from school…something about kids going around saying you're a dyke?"

"That's…that's not true…they're lying, Father!"

"Really? Then what are THESE?" The irate father's voice rumbled as he slammed down the pictures of women and the LGBTQ books the young woman had kept hidden in her room.

"I…"

The father hit the girl.

"You will get these thoughts out of your head! I won't allow it! I won't allow it!"

She knew there was nothing wrong with her. She knew what she was feeling was normal, but there was nothing she could do. The only thing she felt she could do was run and hide.

***

As a child, I hid from my father. Boxed up everything that made me me, just so I wouldn't have to confront my fears. It was easier to pretend I didn't exist.

I've been living in a fantasy the last couple of months; none of it was real. My art wasn't in a museum, I didn't have friends to sit with at lunch, and I don't have a girlfriend. Those things are not me. I'm a loner with no support and no love. Just a loser who hides away and pretends to be someone else.

In some random corner in the vast museum I make myself into a little ball and feel myself sinking lower and lower. I was wrong to give in to my greed, I should have just gone abroad with my parents. I should just always do as my parents tell me…I'm no one…I'm nothing.

Maddy is she crouching in front of me, or maybe she isn't, since she isn't real. Just a fantasy I could never have. She's trying to say something, but nothing is coming out of her mouth…probably because she's not actually real. I close my eyes. If I open them again, she'll probably be gone; that's how it works, right? If you see something not real, you blink a few times and it disappears, but when I close my eyes, I feel something. Something warm and wet pressed against my lips.

I open my eyes and Maddy is staring at me, holding my face. It's strange, I thought you weren't supposed to feel hallucinations?

"I'm real."

My eyes start to focus more, and her voice starts to come in clearer now.

"I'm real, Michelle, we're all real! And we all love you!"

As I stare into Maddy's ocean blue eyes, all the memories starting to flow back into me. The memories I have with Maddy and the boys, the memories of teasing Chloe in class and painting with Sasha, all flood in. As I feel the tears stream down my face, I begin to see my actual reality again. Maddy is real and she is in front of me, and she's concerned.

I hide my head away in shame, a fake smile on my face. "So, what do you think of my parents? Do you think they like you?"

"Michelle…"

"Well, what do you think?" I try to act fine, but the tears won't stop. "You think I'm a coward, right? Unable to speak up to my father, standing still, and running away…"

"That's not…"

"Well, that's me! I'm not this confident cool gay rights activist or anything, I was just living in a fantasy for a short while, that's all. In reality, I'm a coward. Just like my mom."

"You're not a coward…" Maddy does her best to convince me, but at this point I can't even keep my fake smile going.

"Did you not see me out there? I can't do anything! When I'm home, I hide my art away, I pretend to be straight, I have to be everything I'm not! And I'm too much of a coward to do anything else."

Maddy stands up with a stern expression. "You're not a coward." She grabs me and pulls me to my feet. "And you haven't been living in a fantasy here." I stare with a blank expression. She's wrong, I have been living a dream here, an unattainable dream. She grabs my shoulders and shakes them. "Don't you understand! This place is reality! Your parents, they were the fantasy!" I begin to slowly open my eyes more. I'm not really sure what she's saying…my parents are awful, how are they a fantasy? "You've met my parents and you know Paul, they are how real parents are supposed to act. But yours…" She looks me right in the eye. "No parents should act like that. They're not reality, they're a nightmare."

Something clicks in me. Something I was too young and naive to realize as a child. Your parents aren't always right.

"You saved me from an abusive relationship once." Maddy grabs my hands. "It's my turn to save you."

Parents can be wrong. Just because my parents don't let me be myself doesn't mean all parents are like that. Paul, Laurie, Alex, they're not the fake parents, it's my parents. They're not my real...

My eyes widen at the realization. "Maddy!" My smile starts to return as I look upon her face. "Maddy...I..."

"AHHHHHH!" We both look towards the direction of a scream, which is coming from the exhibit hall.

Maddy looks at me, waiting for me, giving me a look that reads, "Take all the time you need." But I'm ready. This has gone on long enough. It's time to end things.

"Let's go." We run together back to the exhibit hall, and what we see is chaos. Sam, Charlie, and Zach are in an all-out brawl. All three are bruised and bloody, but Sam is currently on top of Zach, punching him in the face over and over again. I know I should be concerned, I know I should be stopping them like everyone else is, but I'm so happy seeing Zach get the ever-living shit beat out of him, I don't care. What surprises me most is who I see talking down to my father.

"And who do you think you are to talk about my daughter?"

"I'm Suyeon Park, your daughter's art teacher." Ms. Park stands firm and tall, like always. Even with my dad barking in her face, she doesn't back down.

"Oh, so you're the one who encouraged her to do this?"

"Matter of fact, I went out and found this opportunity just for her."

"Who gave you the right..."

Ms. Park speaks over him. "Your daughter is one of the most talented artists I've ever gotten to know. It would be an absolute shame if her talents were hidden away, not able to shine."

"How…"

"And as an artist myself, may I say that we have a very important and respectful job, and I do not take kindly to you speaking poorly on it."

"Where do you find the nerve…" I see my father begin to raise his hand, but I swoop in and block Ms. Park. "Oh, are you done having a fit? This place is crazy, we are getting out of here."

He turns to leave, but I won't let him. "No."

"Excuse me?"

"No…Father, I…no…George." George's face drops as I use his name. "I've realized something since I've been here. You have never been my father." George starts to stomp over to me but I don't stop. "When have you *EVER* been a father to me?"

"I raised you—"

"Fathers are supposed to be kind, and support their kids!" I look over at Paul, who smiles. "And parents are supposed to accept their kids for who they are, no matter what." I look towards Maddy's parents and give them a nod. "You have never once acted like a real parent to me, and you know what, I'm an adult now. I don't need you in my life."

"You little bitch!" My dad raises his hand, but Paul jumps in front of me and takes the hit. "Paul!"

"You know you shouldn't hit a girl, George."

Eighteen years of hiding who I really am…it needs to end today. "I am proud of who I am, and I've never been ashamed of it. If you have a problem, then you can leave! Goodbye, George." I turn around and start to walk away. George calls after me, but I don't want to give him a final glance.

That is until I hear, "Sir, you're under arrest for destruction of property."

"What?" Hearing how distressed George is, I need to see if what I think is happening is really happening and yep, the police were called and are putting George into handcuffs. "I didn't didn't do shit!"

"You destroyed a painting in this museum with malicious intent. That can be considered a felony." The police officer comes up to me. "Ma'am, that's your painting, correct?" I give a slight nod. "Then, would you like to press charges?"

I look at George, who seems like he's about to explode out of his handcuffs. I turn to the officer and with a sweet smile say, "Abso-fucking-lutely."

The officer nods with a smile and starts leading George away. "No, Michelle! You can't *do* this! Shannon! Do something about our daughter!"

"No." Both George and I are surprised by my mom's response.

"What?"

"I'm done, too!" She explodes in tears. "We destroyed *any* relationship we had with our only daughter! I am *done* being a coward and I am *done* with you. I want a divorce!"

This is a turn of events I did not see coming, but my attention is drawn to Sam and Charlie being put in handcuffs.

"Wait, no!" I try to protest but Sam gives me a reassuring smile.

 "Don't worry, Michelle, we'll be fine."

"But!"

I feel Paul's hand on my shoulder. "It's okay, Michelle, I'll make sure they get out okay."

Paul and I watch as the boys are led away, two in handcuffs, and one on a stretcher. George is eventually led away as well, and my mom slowly approaches me with tears in her eyes.

"I'm so sorry, my baby girl...I could do nothing for you but watch."

I don't respond. I have no words for this woman, but that only makes her cry harder.

"I know I don't deserve your forgiveness. And you don't have to, but I hope someday in the future, you will be willing to let me in your life again." And with that she turns and slowly walks out of the museum.

The museum is a mess at this point. Splattered blood on the floor, a painting torn to shreds, but I am finally able to breathe again. And then I collapse on the ground.

"Michelle!" Everyone runs to me.

Chloe panics. "Michi! Are you okay? I can't believe that stupid asshole! He ruined everything!"

"Shh, Chloe!" Sasha must notice how morose my eyes look.

Chloe quietly whispers, "Oh. Sorry."

Maddy grabs my face. "I'm proud of you."

I reach up and wrap my arms around her neck. "Thanks for saving me there."

She giggles, but then flips her hair in a show-off way. "I know, I'm awesome."

"Pfft, you're ridiculous."

"Ah! But you're smiling now." She has an accomplished grin.

I smile softly. "Yeah, I guess I am."

Sasha grabs my arm. "Come on, let's get you up."

I come up face to face with Ms. Park. She looks like she's struggling to say something, so I speak up first. "Thank you for speaking up to George, Ms. Park. I really appreciate it."

The corners of Ms. Park's mouth turn up ever so slightly. "I'm sorry that your painting got destroyed; it was beautiful."

I wave my hand. "I'll make more." I try to seem fine, but deep down I am really broken about losing it.

"I..." Her face scrunches as she tries to form her words. "I'm not very good at talking to people...so if you've felt that I don't appreciate your work then..."

I cut her off with a hug. She's stunned at first, probably not used to receiving hugs from students, but I want to let her know how much I appreciate her. "Thank you, Ms. Park, thank you for letting my dream come true."

She finally hugs me back. "Just let me know the next time you have a piece in a museum."

I give her a soft "okay" and she bids me farewell. "I'll see you in class on Monday."

As I watch her leave, I feel two sets of arms squeeze my body.

"Oh, dear Michelle! I'm so sorry your parents treated you that way!" Maddy's mom Laurie is crying into me.

"That's right, Michelle, if you need someone, we will adopt you!"

"Honey! We can't adopt her!" Laurie hits her husband. "If she and Maddy are siblings, then how could they be together?"

"Hmm, you're right. Then Maddy just needs to marry Michelle and she'll become our daughter!"

"Oh, that's a great idea!"

"Ugh, no! Mom, Dad, can you go wait in the car, please?"

"Oh fine. Honey, it looks like we're embarrassing Maddy again." Maddy hides her face after her mom's comment. "Michelle, our home is always open to you."

"That's right, please stop by!" I wave goodbye to the Vitises and am left with Sasha, Chloe, Maddy, and Paul.

Maddy starts, "So, how are…"

"Umm actually, I was wondering if I can just go back home…I'm…" I feel my legs wobble. "I'm very tired." I feel like a light switch has flipped and I'm completely shutting down. The weight of the day, of Zach ruining the show, of crying, of confronting my parents…it all comes crashing down on me, and I find myself in a pit surrounded by darkness.

Chapter 24

"Happy birthday to you, happy birthday to you! Happy birthday, dear Maddy! Happy birthday to you!"

Maddy blows out her one and eight candles, and the room flickers with warm, golden light as the celebration commences. All of her friends are there to celebrate, including some of the girls on the cheerleading squad that don't secretly hate her. We're all together to celebrate Maddy's birthday on March 3. March 3, the day the love of my life was born.

"Congrats on finally being an adult!" Chloe says, grabbing Maddy into an embrace.

"Yeah, now that you're eighteen, I can stop feeling awkward about dating a minor." She elbows my stomach.

"You're eighteen like the rest of us." Charlie rests his arm on Maddy's shoulder. "It sucks, doesn't it?" Chloe elbows him in the ribs. But Charlie only smiles and pulls Chloe into a back hug.

"We have this gift for you." Sam walks in carrying a large wrapped present. "We all pitched in to buy it, although some of us pitched in a little more than others," he mumbles under his breath, but we all hear him.

"Hey, I would pitch in more if I had a successful woodwork company!" Charlie has a jealous tone as he speaks. Sam ended up completing the order for the cafe and now he's getting more and more requests each day. He was thinking of dropping out early to start his own company, but Paul said he at least needed a high school degree.

Sam snickers. "Ha, jealous I'll become famous before your band does?"

"Whoa whoa…" The boys playfully fight with each other, their laughter echoing in the air as they engage in a lighthearted tussle. I will never get tired of watching them smile together.

After the museum incident, Sam and Charlie had to be detained for assault, but Paul immediately paid bail. Due to them being first-time offenders, and the fact that Zach deserved it, they wrote it off as a sibling quarrel and the boys were let off with a warning. We were all relieved when they made it home. Chloe and I baked a cake to congratulate them.

"I'm sorry you guys had to go through everything because of me."

"It wasn't because of you, it was because of Zach," Sam says, slicing himself a larger than usual piece of cake.

"Yeah, but you got into a fight because of me."

"Pfft, please," Charlie interrupts, "that fight was a long time coming. I've been holding that punch in for the last five years."

Charlie laughs it off, but I know he's being serious. I think I just sped up what was always bound to happen. Zach was hospitalized. He was alive but barely. He ended up needing a lot of surgery. Paul paid for all of it, not only since he's his son, but also so Zach wouldn't try to sue.

He ended up with a concussion, swollen eyes, and three broken ribs. I'm honestly proud of my boys, I didn't think they had it in them to break ribs, but here we are. Zach's surgery included stitches all over his face which will leave a scar. He also needed to reside in the hospital for several weeks, and is supposed to return home in three days. I know I shouldn't condone violence, but if there was anyone who needed a good beating, it was Zach.

But I enjoy seeing Sam and Charlie happy again, glad they're finally able to live their lives freely.

"Here, open it!" Chloe helps Sam place the box down. "And FYI, it was all Michelle's idea."

"Yep. All me."

"Hey!" Chloe is shocked by my response. "We helped a little!" I laugh with Maddy as she begins tearing the wrapping off.

Maddy gasps and she covers her mouth. "Oh my god, you guys!" She stands up and brings the five of us into a group hug. "This is perfect!"

I've been wanting to get Maddy one for a while, but I didn't have the funds, so we all chipped in together to get her, her very own pale blue sewing machine.

Sasha places another birthday bag in front of Maddy. "We got you some fabric as well, so you can start making clothes as soon as possible."

Maddy's eyes start tearing up. "You guys!"

"Oooh, what's this? A sewing machine!" Laurie walks in with more plates. "Oh Maddy, you must be so happy, you used to make clothes for your Barbies using tissues and tape, and now you can use an actual machine!"

"Mom, don't bring up my embarrassing stories!"

"Why? I think it's cute!" Maddy frowns at me, but I'm just being honest. "When I was younger, I would paint pictures and then hang them around my room like they were in a museum, and then I would walk around admiring them like I was an art critic." Everyone begins laughing. "What? It's not that embarrassing!"

"I know but…" Sam struggles to speak while laughing. "I'm just imagining little Michelle walking around her room like a critic…" Everyone starts laughing more.

"Ugh, whatever, screw you guys."

"No! I think it's cute!" Maddy whispers close to my ears. "You know, after I would make the clothes, I would have my Barbies pretend to be in a fashion show. I would make a little runway to have them walk down."

"Now that is the cutest thing I've ever heard."

Maddy opens the rest of the presents and after that we just watch movies and play card games. Around midnight, Maddy kicks everyone out, except for me, of course, as I'm having a sleepover.

I'm in bed twiddling my thumbs. I need to ask Maddy something in private, and now that we're alone it's the time, but I'm afraid of how she'll react. Maddy gets in and snuggles next to me.

I'm trying to find the courage to ask my question when she says, "Can I ask you something?"

"Uh, sure?" I'm caught off guard. I was about to say the same thing she just did. *Is she a mind reader?*

"Well, I know Zach gets out of the hospital soon." I try to stop myself from groaning at his name, it's kind of become taboo in our group, but I want to hear Maddy out. "I was wondering if, when he gets home, if I could talk to him?"

I only think for a second before saying, "Do you need my permission?"

Maddy raises her eyebrows for a second in shock, but then relaxes and softly giggles. "No, you're right, I don't need your permission."

I once again gather my courage to ask her, "I wanna ask you something too."

"Oh?"

"Well, you said you were going to take a gap year, right? To figure out what you want to do?"

"Yeah, I mean, I'm pretty sure I want to do something with fashion, but, I'm still figuring it out."

"Well, as a painter, I'm always looking for new inspirations, so after I graduate, I am going to use the money I got from the lawsuit against George to renovate a van…that I will then use to travel the country for a year…" I watch Maddy's face, waiting to see if she realizes what I'm asking before I finish, but she's still listening intently, so I continue, "Since you won't be doing anything over the next year…would you like to come with me?" There I said it! I sort of spat it out at the end, but I finally asked her.

Her face starts with a flush of surprise coloring her cheeks, followed by her eyes widening in disbelief. But as she comes to understand what I'm really asking, a shy smile blossoms and an energetic "Yes!" arises from her voice.

I smile and sigh in relief. "Really?"

"Yes, of course!" She pulls me in for a kiss, and I melt into her lips. The world seems to stop in that moment as the warmth of her touch envelops me. We spend the whole night like that, caring for and caressing each other, until we eventually fall asleep, wrapped in each other's warmth. In that moment, everything else in the world goes away, and all that's left is the tranquility of our shared intimacy.

***

Three days later, Maddy arrives with me at the Owens house.

"Do you want me to go in with you?"

"No, but can you stand outside the door?" I nod and let Maddy inside, although she already knows where Zach's room is.

I was worried he might try to hurt her, but after everything, I doubt Zach would even be able to do anything. I don't know why she wants to talk to Zach, she didn't tell me and I didn't ask. I trust Maddy and I know whatever she needs to say will be necessary for her closure.

"Okay, I'm going in." Maddy knocks and waits for Zach's defeated, "Come in."

Like she asked, I stay at the door to listen. I can't hear much but I get the gist of it.

"Because of what I've done, I've lost everything…I lost my looks, my football scholarship…" I remember Paul mentioning the school he signed with canceled the contract after the incident, and apparently that was his only chance of getting into a good school, so now he's applying to any community college that will take him.

"And Maddy, I lost you…"

There's a pause before Maddy "You lost me a long time ago…I hope you realize that. This whole situation…Michelle…you lost me way before all of that happened."

"I know…"

"So what's your plan now?"

"I don't know… My dad mentioned maybe getting professional help, but no matter what I can't go back…after everything I've done. Even if I apologize it won't be enough."

"You're right. You can't go back. So you just have to go forward… And I want you to know that I will not be in your future. This is probably the last day you will ever see me again." Maddy is surprisingly calm and professional the whole time talking to Zach; she doesn't falter at all. "I wanted to come see you to say goodbye. Thank you for being a part of my life, but I'm ready to move on, and I don't see you in my life going forward. Farewell, Zach."

I hear Maddy's footsteps walking out, but Zach calls after her, "I know Michelle is out there, can you ask her to come in? I wanna talk to her real quick."

Before Maddy can respond, I walk in. As much as I never wanted to talk to Zach again, I also want closure. You can only open a new book once you close the old one, so I want it to be over with Zach.

Zach is sitting in a wheelchair, his face reformed, and he looks like a deflated old man. "Michelle, I know it won't matter at all but I'm sorry. With what I did to you, I ended up losing everything…and the only person I have to blame is myself… So, I know this won't fix anything, but I just need to say sorry."

I breathe and let my body find calm. I want to handle this with sincerity. "Zach, I understand you're sorry, and I accept that, but I will not forgive you. I am going to move on with my life, and I will just never spare you a thought again. After this moment, you no longer exist to me. Thank you."

Without hearing his response I turn and leave the room. Maddy follows after me. We hear him begin to cry, the regret of his actions weighing heavily on him as he finally understands how much he's lost.

Maddy and I drive to our special field and have a celebratory picnic. With our thoughts about Zach resolved, we are officially ready to start a new stage in life, one filled with new stories and unknown possibilities. Our story is just beginning, and now with our hands intertwined, we embark on a new journey.

Chapter 25

"Hey, Michelle, where do you want this?" Sam holds up a few of my extra canvases.

"There should be some extra space in the bottom drawer under the bed. If not, just put them up front for now." I look over at the rest of my friends who were supposed to be helping. "Hey, we still have a lot of stuff to pack! Some help would be nice!"

"Oh, come on! Sorting through your photos is just as important. Like, you have to take this one of Charlie and I winning prom king and queen."

Maddy snatches the photo from her hand. "We're good, you guys can keep this one. Hey, Charlie, come grab your prom photo before Chloe stuffs it into my luggage!"

Charlie drops his guitar and runs over. "That wasn't supposed to be in the pile, I got that to put in my guitar case."

"Oh oops…sorry."

"It's okay, babe." Charlie kisses Chloe and puts the photo in his case. "I'm just going to run this up to my room and then I'll be down to help."

"Oh god, look at our graduation photo." Sasha holds up a photo of all of us in matching navy blue gowns. "I hate that we're all looking in a different direction."

I run over to the girls. If they're not going to help yet, then I might as well reminisce. "Graduation was so boring."

I barely remember it. It was long, we were hot outside, and it's not like any of my dumbass friends were valedictorian. The only good part was Maddy's party which featured Charlie's band.

"How about this photo?"

Sasha hands me a photo of the two of us and Ms. Park, who is showing one of her rare smiles. Ms. Park ended up being my favorite teacher. Even if she didn't talk much, she would still listen to me and give me helpful tips. If I showed her a painting I was working on, she would always stop what she was doing to analyze it. I'm glad I was able to get to know her better.

"By the way, Sash, what school did you end up picking?" I ask. "You got accepted to so many."

"California Institute of Art. I got a scholarship so…"

"But you'll be so far away from us!" Chloe says, while holding her. "What am I going to do without you?"

"Come visit me."

Chloe doesn't like that answer. "But it's so far!"

Charlie finally joins the conversation. "It's okay, babe, once we start touring with our band, we'll go to California first, okay?"

Chloe pouts a bit before saying a shy "okay."

"And you two better be in California at that time, too, okay?"

I roll my eyes. "Yeah, yeah, we will…"

"Chloe, how did your parents react when you told them you weren't going to college?" Maddy asks with a curious expression.

"They weren't surprised. Actually, they told me they thought I wouldn't be able to get into college even if I did apply…" Chloe pouts again. "I know I'm bad at studying but still."

Charlie wraps his arms around Chloe. "But we're grateful to have you help us on the road. Without you, I'd get so lonely." Charlie buries his face into her neck.

"I know, I know." She turns and gives him a kiss.

"Hey, if you guys wanna stop flirting and help me finish packing the van that *you*"—he looks at me and Maddy—"are going to be traveling in, that would be great."

Everyone groans as they get up, saying, "Fine…" and, "Okay…" We spend the rest of the afternoon packing up clothes, essentials, food, and whatever else we'll need. We throw around supplies as we talk about the past year and the adventures yet to come. By the afternoon, the van is packed and Maddy and I are set to leave in the morning.

"So, what time are you going to be leaving tomorrow?" Chloe asks, her lip already quivering.

"Probably around five. We wanna beat rush hour traffic and such."

Chloe's lip quivers even more as a tear starts rolling down her cheek. "Then I guess this is goodbye?"

"Well…" Chloe pulls me into a hug as I start to tear up. "Remember this isn't goodbye, it's just see you later."

Chloe sniffles. "Okay." She lets go and her eyes are bright red, full of tears. Seeing her usual chipper self look so sad makes me start to bawl.

"Damn it, Chloe, I said I wasn't going to cry yet here I am crying!" She laughs as she wipes the tears from her face.

Next up Sasha pulls me in for a hug. "Thank you for keeping me company in the art room. I was afraid it was going to be another boring year of sitting at an easel and painting, but you made it fun." Sasha's crying as well, but she is trying to hide it.

"I'll miss your guessing what your next hair color will be…" We all had a bet on which color she was going to choose. I guessed rainbow, but she went with pink.

She snorts. "Just make sure you come visit me in Cali, okay?"

"Of course."

Maddy begins to say her goodbyes to the girls and I am left with Sam and Charlie.

"Why the hell are you boys crying? We're having dinner tonight together, this isn't goodbye."

"I know but…" Charlie starts wiping his eyes. "To think this will be the last time all six of us are together for a while…"

I hadn't thought about that yet. "Thank you, Charlie, for making me cry more."

Sam pulls us both in. "Michelle, thank you for everything, and thank you for being our little sister."

"Yeah, you're the best younger sibling I've ever had."

I give Charlie the "seriously?" stare before going back into the hug.

We stay like this for a while. I wish we could stay forever, but it's getting late and the sun is going away.

"Maddy, Michelle, go in the van, I want to take photos for my website." Sam did about 99 percent of the work on the van. He wants to spread his business to more than just woodwork, and I think he'll do it.

"Now, everyone in for the group photo!" Sam runs inside and we all mumble and mush together. Sam comes out with Paul.

"Oh, I can't believe you're all packed and ready to go!" Paul stands back and holds the camera ready. "Everyone smile!" As he takes our photo, I notice tears in Paul's eyes. It seems everyone is crying over us leaving. I had only spent a year here, yet I made so many friends who care for me and cry for me.

So much has changed in a year, and now Maddy and I are about to spend a year on the road. Who knows what else will change?

Made in the USA
Middletown, DE
25 January 2025

70238182R00139